Unruly Son

Neil S. Plakcy

This book is a work of fiction. Names, characters, places, and incidents either are products of the author's imagination or are used fictitiously. Any resemblance to actual events or locales or persons, living or dead, is entirely coincidental.

Copyright 2020 by Neil S. Plakcy All rights reserved, including the right of reproduction in whole or in part in any form.

Cover by Kelly Nichols, Editing by Randall Klein

Establishing the chronology of the novels is tricky because *Mahu Men: Mysterious and Erotic Stories,* and *Accidental Contact: Mahu Investigations,* fill in the gaps between novels. Here's the way I organize the whole series:

Mahu
Mahu Surfer
- A finalist for the 2007 *Lambda Literary Award for Best Gay Mystery*
Mahu Fire
- A finalist for the 2008 *Lambda Literary Award for Best Gay Mystery*
- Winner of the 2008 *Left Coast Crime award for Best Police Procedural*
Mahu Vice
Mahu Men: Mysterious and Erotic Stories
Mahu Blood
Zero Break
Natural Predators
Accidental Contact and Other Mahu Investigations
Children of Noah
Ghost Ship
Deadly Labors
Soldier Down
Unruly Son

This book is licensed to the original purchaser only. Duplication or distribution via any means is illegal and a violation of International Copyright Law, subject to criminal prosecution and upon conviction, fines and/or imprisonment. This eBook cannot be legally loaned or given to others. No part of this eBook can be shared or reproduced without the express permission of the publisher.

"Unruly sun, why dost thou thus," – John Donne, "The Sun Rising"

Chapter 1
Invasive Species

I stabbed a cherry tomato right in the center as a dribble of juice spurted out. Then I threaded a white button mushroom onto the skewer behind it, followed by a slice of limp green pepper. It felt good to get my frustrations out after a week on the homicide beat by annihilating these vegetables, then imagining the skewers charring on the backyard grill.

I realized I was getting too into kitchen violence, and shifted to forming a platter of roughly-rounded hamburger patties. I tried not to think of the way the raw meat resembled brain matter. But when you're a cop, it's hard to leave your work behind.

Fortunately my sweetheart came in then, and all thoughts of death and destruction flew out the window. I still believed Mike Riccardi was the handsomest man I knew. Six-four, with broad shoulders and wavy black hair and an oval face with dark eyes that shone. He was an assistant chief in the Honolulu Fire Department, the kind of man who ran toward danger rather than away from it.

I was the same kind of guy, and though we had come to accept that about each other, I still worried every time I heard a fire siren. At least I was comfortable with him around a grill.

He picked up one of the cherry tomatoes and popped it into his mouth, and I was mesmerized for a moment by the movement of his mustache as he chewed. "I thought you started the grill already," I said.

"I did. I want to get the coals nice and red."

"Who's watching it?"

"Dakota."

I looked through the window at the yard behind our house. Under the umbrella of a monkeypod tree, our twenty-three-year-old foster son, Dakota Gianelli, was leaning against a tree facing the back of our yard, his phone to his ear. Then behind him, a giant ball of flame burst from the grill. "Oh, shit," Mike said, and dashed back there. "Dakota!"

We had taken Dakota in when he was a teen, and he had grown into a solid young man, his Italian heritage evident in his Mediterranean skin, dark hair and Roman nose. Too bad he didn't have enough sense to watch an open flame.

I carried the platter outside. Mike had turned the grill way down and stood at the ready with a fire extinguisher. "I said I'm sorry," Dakota said.

"Sorry I didn't burn the house down," Mike said.

"At least we know we raised a lousy arsonist," I said.

A flight of green parrots with bright red heads surprised us by zooming out of the tree cover and over our heads. Like the ironwood, they were an invasive species that had made a home in the Aloha State. The same was true for Dakota, born in New Jersey and brought to Honolulu by his mother when she was fleeing bad guys back home.

The same could even be true for Mike, whose father was Italian-American from New York, and his Korean-born mother. They had come to Hawai'i when Mike was a kid to escape prejudice against mixed marriages on Long Island.

The smell of grilled meat rose, and our golden retriever, Roby, positioned himself beside Mike, waiting for his first tidbit. Dakota's phone rang, but he shut it off and stuck it in his pocket. When Mike handed him the first burger off the grill, he busied himself doctoring it with lettuce, tomato, mayonnaise and a large squirt of Korean hot sauce, a taste he'd acquired from Mike.

It was a lovely Sunday evening, and I didn't even have to put on music because someone a few houses down was playing a concert by Kalani Pe'a, a young singer with the pipes of a belter, folded into soothing island rhythms.

Mike pulled burgers off the grill for the two of us, and I loaded up a platter of grilled vegetable skewers.

"How's your work?" Dakota asked me as we ate.

"Must be something in the stars," I said. "One weird case after another. A man attacked his neighbors with roach spray because their music was too loud. Another guy threatened to destroy the world with an army of turtles. We picked up a drunk who was eating spaghetti with his bare hands at an Italian restaurant on Waikiki. And another guy had this scam going where he held a lemonade packet in his hand and used that on the self-checkout at the Walmart each time he scanned a more expensive item."

"That's inventive," Mike said. "And less violent than using a gun, right?"

Then Dakota said, "Um, speaking of criminals. My mom called me last week and asked if I would come to see her." His normally handsome face was contorted.

Dakota knew we had a low opinion of his mother because of her history with drugs and crime, but I had to admit he was a sharp kid, leading the conversation in a way that let him drop his bombshell. I leaned forward in my lawn chair. "Did you?"

Mike put his hand on my arm, a warning not to get too angry too quickly. "Kimo," he said. We were nearly the same age, though most people would say he was way more level-headed than I was. We both had eyes with a slight slant and favored aloha shirts when not at work, but he was a few inches taller than I was and broader in the chest.

I took a deep breath, and Dakota nodded.

"I drove up to Wahiawa on Thursday when I had the afternoon

off." Dakota's tone was deliberately conversational, though the subject had all three of us on edge. His mom had been at The Women's Community Correctional Center, in the center of the island, for as long as I'd known him.

"How's she doing?" Mike asked.

Dakota looked up. "Better. They have her in a vocational rehab program preparing her to get out."

I didn't like the sound of that. "When would she be released?"

"As long as she behaves, right after the first of the year," Dakota said. "She's going to a halfway house in Kaneohe for a while until she gets her bearings." He looked down again. "She wants us to get a place together."

"In Kaneohe?" I asked.

He shook his head. "On the Leeward Coast, near where I work. She's been learning customer service and cash management skills. She could get a service job at one of the hotels. Maybe even the Disney property."

"How do you feel about that, Dakota?" Mike asked.

I was glad he brought it up because my heart was racing with anger toward Angelina Gianelli and I couldn't have made the question sound as casual as Mike did.

"I don't know what to think," he said, and I could hear the anguish in his voice. "I mean, what do I owe her? She was a lousy mom and she basically abandoned me when she started doing drugs. I was on my own long before she went to prison."

I couldn't argue with that.

"She says I'm a bad son because I haven't been to see her enough, because I'm not out there working to get her released. As if I could. And now I need to make it up to her by helping her out."

"It's a tough situation," Mike said. "You know you're always welcome here. But your mom?" He shook his head. "I think the K-Man and I both agree that we don't want anything to do with her."

"But she doesn't have anyone else!" Dakota said. "My grandparents are too old and they gave up on her years ago. She has a brother and a sister back in Jersey but neither of them will even accept a collect call from her."

"There are lots of people who have to make their way in the world on their own," I said, trying to stay calm. As a beat cop for years in Waikiki, and then a homicide detective in downtown Honolulu, I had met all kinds of people, victims and villains alike. "I see it all the time. You screw over everyone who cares about you and…" I took a breath. "At least she's got the halfway house, and she's getting some skills."

I stood up and started pacing around the yard. "You need to tell her she has to prove herself to you. Let her get a job and a place to live, and be sober and employed for a year. Then think about moving in together if she still wants to."

"We can't tell you what to do," Mike said, with a sharp glance at me. "You have a brain and a heart, and while it may take you a while to process everything, eventually you'll make the decision that's right for you."

There was a lot more I wanted to say on the topic, but one look from Mike and I shut my mouth. The three of us ate quietly, as the music in the background changed from Kalani Pe'a to Paula Fuga's smoky voice wondering if ever she could see someone again, and what would happen.

"We had some weird stuff of our own at the fire department this week," Mike said after a while. Dakota and I both looked up from eating.

"Woman cleaning out her grandfather's house on the North Shore found a World War II grenade and she brought it to the Sunset Beach station," he continued. "Grenade still had a pin in it, so we had to evacuate the station and call in the bomb squad."

"Was it still live after all these years?" Dakota asked.

"That's what the technician said. And then the guys at Pearl City had to remove a man's penis from a hole in his bowling ball where it got stuck."

"Ouch," I said. "And embarrassing, too." I turned to Dakota. "See, there are some places you just shouldn't stick your dick."

He laughed. "I'll remember that."

When we finished eating, I carried the plates inside and loaded the dishwasher while Mike and Dakota scrubbed the grill. When I was back in my chair again, I asked Dakota, "How are you doing, kiddo?"

Dakota took a deep breath. "Better. I know you say I don't listen to you enough, but I'm going to take your advice. Push my mom off for a while, see how things develop."

I nodded. There was nothing more I could do to help Dakota, at least not until the State of Hawai'i's plans for his mother were more definite.

Chapter 2
Guest Suite

My cell phone rang, and I was surprised to see my old friend Ray Donne's name on the display. He had been my detective partner for years until he and his wife returned to Philadelphia, and he was as much family to me as my brothers, my cousins, or Mike and Dakota. "Aloha, bud. Calling with early Christmas wishes?"

"Well, that too," he said. "Wanted to give you the news as quick as I had it. We're coming back to Honolulu."

I was stunned. A pueo, or short-eared owl, swooped through the trees and I looked up, as if Ray was there. "Back here? Why?"

He laughed. "Don't sound so excited."

I watched as the owl swooped down to the ground and grabbed a mouse in its beak, then flapped its wings back up to the tree canopy and disappeared from sight. "I thought you and Julie wanted to be closer to your family."

"So did we. But we underestimated a couple of things. The availability of her parents and mine to babysit, for one thing." In the background I heard his son Vinnie, who was 10, arguing with his mother.

"And?"

"And we got spoiled by the weather out there, and Julie hates her job here, so she reached out to the guy at UH who mentored her, Joshua Kalani Walsh. Turns out he had a heart attack in August, just before the school year started. Decided to retire. They advertised for someone to replace him, and lucky for us, they didn't get many qualified applicants."

"Except Julie?"

"Except Julie. Walsh is in the middle of a big longitudinal study of Pacific Islanders, and Julie spent three years of her PhD as his assistant, so she knows the study backwards and forwards. And the last year or so, she's been working in marketing research for a consulting firm, and one of her biggest clients was Hawaiian Airlines, analyzing data about why people come to the islands and what they do. Her work piggybacks onto his, so it's a perfect addition for the department."

I laughed. "You don't have to sell her to me, Ray. She's a star and I've always known it."

"She's had a hell of a time getting a job teaching Asian and Pacific Islander studies since she is neither Asian nor a Pacific Islander, so the timing of this is a godsend. She had a couple of Zoom interviews and yesterday afternoon they called and said yes."

"That's great, bud. When do you get here?"

"We're flying out tonight. That's the thing I'm hoping you can help with. We're only renting here—we stopped looking to buy when we realized Julie was so unhappy. Our landlord will let us out of the lease January 1. But I don't know how we're going to find something we can afford in Honolulu in the middle of tourist season."

"Let me ask around," I said. "I may know people who know people."

It was true; O'ahu was one island, and my family, friends and Punahou classmates were spread all over it. Half of the time when I'm investigating a case, I know someone who knows someone I can talk to.

I told him I was excited to see him, Julie and Vinnie, and ended the call. The first people I thought to ask were Mike's and my baby mamas.

I had known Sandra Guarino and her wife, Cathy Selkirk, for years before they approached Mike and me to donate sperm so they could have a child. Sandra was a prominent attorney in Honolulu, and though she didn't often take criminal cases, our paths had crossed periodically.

A year before, Sandra had been asked by the governor to fill a seat in the US House of Representatives vacated by the unfortunate death of a woman who had made a lot of enemies. Sandra, who had spent her career making alliances across courtrooms and party lines, was a great choice. The previous fall, she had won election to her own two-year term.

A paddled ceiling fan in our living room swirled cool air, and even with the lights off I could find my way to our newest purchase, a leather sofa with a recliner at one end. I settled into the chair, raised my feet up, and checked my email for the weekly schedule Cathy sent out to family and friends, a coordination of the days the House was in session, the Punahou school schedule, and any trips they had planned.

Sandra was in DC, and five hours ahead of us. Good. I could catch her before she went to sleep. "Hey, little mama, how you doing?" I asked when she answered her phone, in a faux-Jersey accent I had learned from Dakota.

"You know I hate it when you call me that."

"But secretly you love it. You love being the mother of those two adorable twins."

"That I'll agree with. What's up?"

"You remember my ex-partner, Ray, and his wife Julie? Julie nabbed a teaching job at UH so they're coming back. They need some short-term housing. You know anyone who'd rent out to a cop, a professor and a ten-year-old?"

"I'd have to verify with Cathy, but you know we have that guest suite out by the pool. It's small, but there are two bedrooms and a living room with a galley kitchen."

"I thought you were fixing that up so that Cathy's parents could come and stay for a while."

"They're happy in Oregon," Sandra said. "They like it when we stop over there when we're flying between DC and Honolulu."

"In other words they love their grandchildren, but in small doses."

"Can you blame them? Those babies came out of my uterus like a railroad train and I love them more than life itself, but every time I get on a plane to DC and leave them behind I feel this deep sigh of relief."

"Hey, you're talking about my kids there," I said, though I knew what she was talking about. At nine years old Addie and Owen had developed their own personalities and yet retained a twinned connection that provided a formidable opponent when they didn't get what they wanted.

"How is Julie and Ray's son? Well-behaved?"

"Honestly, I haven't asked. But he always wants books for birthday and Christmas gifts, so that's a good sign."

"I'll call Cathy and talk it through with her and one of us will call you back."

I thanked her and hung up. Then I sat back and closed my eyes. It would be great to have Ray back, hopefully as my partner once more. We had always been a great team, at HPD and then when we'd gone on special assignment to the FBI. It was when we were ready to return to regular policing that he and Julie had decided it was a good time to go back home.

Home, however, is not always what you think it will be.

Cathy's cell number showed up on my phone a few minutes later. "They can move in whenever they want," she said. "Just give us a day's notice."

"Better yet, I'll give Julie your number and cut out the middleman."

"Works for me."

"Thanks, Cathy. I appreciate it. With luck, the kids will get along, and you'll feel comfortable having a cop in the back yard when Sandra is away."

"Is he going back to HPD?" she asked.

"That's my next project."

I called Ray back and gave him the good news. "For real?" he asked. "That quick?"

"Hey, you know me. Bull in a china shop. Never stop to consider the impact of my actions."

"You won't get any argument from me. I really appreciate it, Kimo. This makes everything so much easier."

"What about you? You going to try for your old job back?"

"What's it like these days?"

"Steve Hart is moving back to California," I said. "Big going away party for him next week. If you get here in time, you should come."

"Any news on who's replacing him?"

"Mary Luo from the Chinatown substation," I said. "But with budget cutbacks I don't have a steady partner. We'd have to tackle Lieutenant Sampson, see what he can work out."

Chapter 3
Death of a Legend

While I was sleeping Sunday night, I got a text message from Ray that they were waiting for the rental car shuttle at Honolulu International Airport, a few minutes after midnight. He thanked me for the connection to Cathy and Sandra, and said he'd be in touch once they got some shuteye.

On Monday, I wanted to talk to my boss, Lieutenant Jim Sampson, about Ray, but I missed him by minutes. When I arrived at the Alapai Headquarters in downtown Honolulu at eight o'clock, Sampson had already been in and left for a meeting of the department's top brass.

I spent the morning on paperwork but had to leave at noon for an appointment at the Medical Examiner's Office. I was on my way out of the building, passing the lei-covered memorial to officers who died in the line of duty, when I spotted Sampson across the street, accompanied by a pair of other lieutenants. I tried to hail him but he was deep in conversation, and I had to get to the morgue.

The ME's office was in a low-slung white building in an industrial neighborhood of Iwilei, behind the Salvation Army. Sadly anyone who came there for an autopsy was beyond salvation.

The receptionist, Alice Kanamura, had been behind the front

desk for as long as I'd been going there, and despite the grimness of my visits she had always been a cheerful sunny presence. That day, though, she looked sad.

"What's up Alice?" I asked. "You okay?"

"My mom passed away last week. Because she was home alone when she died, she had to have an autopsy. I know Doc was gentle with her, because that's the way he is. But every time I think of her in there being cut open I get sad."

"I'm so sorry," I said. "My dad used to say that he wanted to die quietly in his sleep, not screaming like the passengers in the car with him."

Alice's eyes widened, and then she laughed.

"In the end, he went the way your mom did, in his sleep at home. I can't imagine how hard that was for my mom, but she said she preferred to think of him in heaven, on a surfboard, where she knew he was happy."

"My mom loved to quilt." Alice showed me a shawl-sized piece of fabric made of quilted squares in a bird of paradise pattern. I saw the careful stitching of each leaf and flower. "I have this here when I get cold."

"It's beautiful," I said. "Imagine her in heaven, quilting these for the angels. I'm sure that would make her very happy."

"It would. She made baby quilts, you know, to give to poor women. When I get sad I think of all those babies sheltered in her love."

She smiled. "Doc is waiting for you in his office. You can go on back."

When I first met our Medical Examiner, Paul "Doc" Takayama, twelve or thirteen years before, he was only in his late twenties, a med school prodigy who looked impossibly young. He'd gone into pathology, he said, so that he wouldn't have to keep justifying his age to patients.

Now, he looked more mature, though he still had a baby face. And some of the awkwardness of his youth had faded away, too. He didn't conduct every autopsy himself, but he'd taken on this one, which had several contradicting problems. The case had come in from the North Shore, a surfer who had hit his head on rocks at Banzai Pipeline, a surf spot with one of the deadliest wave patterns in the world.

The surf, often strong, broke over shallow water by a sharp reef, and it took an experienced surfer to manage it. Doc had called me in because of my surfing experience—in addition to a life spent on the water, I had tried to make it on the pro circuit for nearly a year before changing direction and heading to the police academy.

"What's up, Doc?" I asked, as I walked into the autopsy suite. Immediately I was assailed by the odor, and pulled a tube of Vick's Vapo-Rub from my pocket, a trick I had learned years before. A quick swipe beneath my nose helped with the smell.

"I want your opinion on these bruises," he said. That was definitely a shift; usually I was asking Doc for medical advice.

He lifted a white sheet from the foot of a body on an examining table. The bottoms of both feet had been sliced up. "Looks like coral," I said. "I've done that to myself a couple of times."

I stared at the feet and thought. "Hold on, it doesn't make sense that he'd hit the coral feet first," I said. "The way Pipeline breaks, he'd be more likely to get knocked into the water and then bounced over the coral. Are there bruises on his side, too?"

He lifted the sheet further and I peered in. "Yeah, these are what I'd expect. I still have a wicked scar on my right side from a coral encounter when I was younger and stupider."

I looked up at Doc. "But that doesn't explain the bruises on his feet. He'd have to have fallen off his board and slid feet-first into the coral. Did anyone see him fall?"

Doc shook his head. "It was early in the morning, just after dawn, and not many surfers were out. A couple getting into their wetsuits spotted him on the sand and called the police."

"Something made him fall," I said. "You know anything about him? A good surfer?"

"Just his name and address, from ID found in his car. Frederic Corsetti. Haleiwa resident."

"Freddy Corsetti?" I said. "He's a legend, Doc. A dozen or more championships under his belt." I pulled out my phone. "Let me check the surf report for Pipeline this morning."

I read through it. "Nothing unusual, no rip current. Wave heights are hovering in the waist to stomach high range. Those should be a breeze for a surfer like Freddy. Did you run a blood test?"

"He exhibits some evidence of thallium poisoning, but there isn't enough in his blood to kill him."

"Doesn't thallium leave the body quickly?"

"It does. So I did a microscopic analysis of a hair and its root. The results showed a tapered follicle with a black root, which is pathognomonic for thallium toxicity. I wanted to get your opinion before I get the North Shore CSI to confiscate everything in his kitchen and start that whole run of tests."

I thought for a minute. "Isn't thallium easily brought in through the skin?"

"It is. But you'd have to swim in it to get enough concentration." Doc's mouth dropped open. "Could there be something in the water? Illegal dumping?"

I shook my head. "He was wearing a wetsuit, right? And standing on a board? His body wouldn't have that much exposure to the water, even when he was swimming out to catch a wave."

We looked at each other, and at the same time, we both said, "Wetsuit."

"If someone rubbed crushed thallium tablets on the inside of his wetsuit, the chemical ought to interact with his sweat and the water to knock him out, right? And that would be consistent with falling from his board and hitting the coral feet first."

"I have some tests to run," Doc said. "Thanks, Kimo."

"You've done me a million favors," I said. "Glad to do one for you."

I was happy to be able to help Doc, but eager to get back to headquarters and catch Lieutenant Sampson. Unfortunately, I had to be in court to testify in a case from the previous year, and I had to wait hours to be called. By the time I returned to the office, Sampson had already left for the day.

I couldn't blame him, but Steve Hart had stopped pulling his weight as his departure approached, and though Mary Luo was an experienced detective, she didn't know our district well enough yet. As the holidays approached and tourists flooded O'ahu, the rate of crime increased, and the rest of us were working flat out. I hadn't had a full-time partner since Ray left, because Sampson thought I was experienced enough to work on my own.

But I wanted that to change now that Ray was back in the picture.

Chapter 4
Missing Persons

Tuesday morning I woke to a phone message, an alert for an all-hands meeting at eight, and even though I got there early, Sampson was on the phone and only came out of his office to address the squad room, filled with on and off-duty detectives and patrol officers.

"Thanks for coming in," he began. He was a big, broad-shouldered haole, or white, who had played minor-league baseball in his youth and retained an athletic build. "We have a missing persons case, and the trail is already cold. I need every pair of eyes on the street looking for this mother and son."

He hit a couple of buttons on his remote, and the room lights dimmed as the projector kicked in. "This is Karen D'Arcy Fontenot," he said as a photo of a middle-aged woman with elegantly cut brown hair appeared on the screen. "Caucasian female, forty-nine years old. Five-nine, approximately one hundred forty pounds. No identifying tattoos though she does have a slight scar from a Caesarean birth."

He clicked the screen, and a photo of a sullen young man appeared. "She is believed to be with her son, Charles D'Arcy Fontenot, age fourteen. Though you can't tell from this shot, he has those clear braces on his teeth..."

"Invisalign," Mary Luo said. When she set up her desk, I saw a photo of her with her husband and a teenaged daughter with braces. I could only imagine how much it would cost if both Addie and Owen needed them.

"Thank you," Sampson said. "Approximately one hundred pounds. Surgical scars from a broken right wrist and elbow." He took a breath. "Charles was diagnosed with Asperger's Syndrome at age three. He is said to lack verbal skills and is easily moved to physical violence."

"Great," muttered someone in the room.

"Karen and Charles arrived in Honolulu on Thursday night, accompanied by six other members of their immediate family. They are staying in several suites at the Albergo d'Italia, a new luxury resort in Kahala."

He flipped to the next slide, a property in the same chain as the one where Dakota was working on the Leeward Coast. "Karen took Charles on morning hikes starting on Friday, returning each day by noon to spend time with the rest of the family," Sampson continued. "Yesterday morning, they left the hotel and did not return."

Mary Luo raised her hand. "Why wasn't this reported yesterday?"

"Good question. According to her brother Jules, who reported her missing, she is a very independent and high-strung individual who did not like to have her choices questioned, especially with regard to her son. When she didn't return for lunch, Jules and the rest of the family assumed that Charles was acting up and Karen was keeping him somewhere until he calmed down."

I began to get bad feelings about this case. A high-strung mother, an unruly son, unsupportive relatives. But I waited to say anything until I heard the full story.

"What about the father?" I asked. "Is he at the hotel, too?"

"According to Karen's brother, the birth father is not in the picture," Sampson said. He turned back to the screen, which showed a bar graph over time. "We all know the numbers. There are currently about 7,500 missing persons in Hawai'i. Let's do our best to rescue Karen and Charles from that list."

Then he brought up a map of the Kahala area. "District 6 will be handling interviews of the hotel staff. Their personnel will search the hotel grounds and all the way down to Wai'alae Beach Park. They have asked for our assistance canvassing homes along Kahala Avenue as far as Black Point."

Someone groaned. That was a long stretch to cover.

"I'll need cars to survey the parking areas of Diamond Head and the various trailheads within a few miles of the hotel. It's possible that she drove somewhere to hike and is currently in distress."

He read out assignments from a list. "Kanapa'aka, you grew up near there, so you probably know all the trailheads and parking areas best. I want you on that."

At least I wouldn't be on foot, I thought, though it would take a lot of navigating to hit all the right places. Sampson handed out sheets with photos of mother and son and their relevant information, and then walked back to his office.

I got there just as he was about to shut his door. "Lieutenant, can I talk to you for a minute?"

He looked at his watch. "Just a minute. I'm due in a meeting."

"Ray Donne is back in Honolulu and needs a job, and I need a partner."

He looked at me in surprise. "That was quick and concise. Somewhat unlike you."

"Well, you said you only had a minute."

"You know the budget is tight." Sampson pursed his lips together. "Although."

I knew the man well enough to wait for his thoughts to crystallize.

"I've been in meetings for the last couple of days with the mayor and various representatives of tourism agencies. This current situation doesn't sit well with them. This might be the right time to bring in the extra detective we need. Can he get in here this afternoon? Say three-thirty?"

"I'll make sure of it, sir." I hurried away before he could change his mind.

I went to my desk and pulled up a map of the Windward Coast, zooming in on Kahala. Then in another window I searched for a hiker's guide to the area. I began listing every place Karen might have driven to begin a hike, even the small neighborhood parks. Wherever possible I copied out an actual street address I could put into my GPS.

The room began to empty as officers and sergeants and detectives headed out to begin their search. I printed everything I had, went out to my Jeep, and plugged the first destination in.

While I drove, I used my Bluetooth to call Ray. He sounded groggy when he answered. "You all right, brah?"

"Took a nap. This time change is killing me."

"Well, wake up, sunshine. You've got an appointment with Sampson this afternoon at three-thirty to talk about getting your old job back."

"You move fast."

"You know me. Push my way into things without thinking them through."

"In this case I'll hold my complaints," he said. "Jesus, really? Three-thirty?"

"I suggest you look up everything you can find about this case we've got going, a missing mother and son. Be ready to tell Sampson what you can do to help. Didn't you tell me you took a bunch of courses on how to deal with kids with behavioral issues? Because that's exactly what we need."

"I've got my notes packed away somewhere. I'll dig them up." He paused for a second. "I really owe you, Kimo. First the house and now a job?"

"It's what you'd do for me, brah. See you later."

My next call was to Terri Hirsch, my best female friend since our days at Punahou, when she and our friend Harry Ho and I were inseparable. Too much time and too many responsibilities kept us farther than we liked, but I was heading to her neighborhood.

"Aloha, stranger," she said, when she answered. "How's everything going?"

"Too many crazy things at once," I said. "Good news is that Ray and Julie have returned from Philadelphia, and for now moving into the guest house behind Cathy and Sandra's place. Addie and Owen are getting their old friend back."

"So are you. Is he coming back to HPD?"

Terri's first husband, long gone, had been a cop, so she knew the special demands of the police force. "Not sure yet. They're meeting this afternoon."

I paused, thinking about how to say what I wanted. "So there's a BOLO for a mother and child who may be in your neighborhood." I told her about Karen and Charles Fontenot. "If you were taking Danny out for a hike—that is, before he graduated from Punahou, headed off to Harvard and left you an empty nester—where would you have gone?"

"Thank you for that brief recap of the last few years of my life," she said, laughing. "Let me think for a minute."

There was a comfortable silence between us as I got onto the H1 highway, heading toward Diamond Head. On O'ahu, we rarely use the directions east, west, north or south. I was heading roughly east, in the direction of the extinct volcano that loomed over the bottom of the Windward Coast.

"Do you know if she preferred the mountains or the beach?" Terri asked.

"No idea. Have to check them all. Though other officers have been assigned to check out Diamond Head."

"Then I'd go to Koko Head first. If I was a tourist, I'd want to see the beach and you know as well as I do there are some gorgeous views there." She suddenly caught her breath. "Has there been a rip tide there lately?"

I knew what she was getting at. Mom and son go into the water, which looks beautiful and safe, and get caught in a strong, localized, and narrow current of water which moves directly away from the shore, cutting through the lines of breaking waves like a river running out to sea. That would explain why they hadn't come home.

"I'll call Harry. He can bring up the surf report for me."

"Good idea. If you don't find their car there, then I'd circle back to the Wiliwilinui Hiking Trail."

"I know it. Mike and I went there a year or so ago. Very steep, though it sounds like she's an experienced hiker."

I thanked Terri and as the H1 transitioned into the Kalaniana'ole Highway, with the attendant slowdown at the first traffic light, I called Harry.

"This is a rare treat," he said, when he answered.

"I know. I got the same shtick from Terri when I called her."

"What is this? Phone a friend day? Or do you need something?"

"Both." I paused, and remembered the manners that my mother had tried, without much luck, to drill into me, and which Terri had reinforced all through our teen years.

The three of us made an unlikely trio. She was the patrician daughter of wealth, and she provided the emotional insight that males such as Harry and I were often lacking. Harry was a brilliant computer geek, holder of a dozen patents, who was as dedicated a surfer as I was during our years at Punahou.

I was the guy who came up with the ideas and then pushed through until Terri and Harry followed. Terri concocted elaborate excuses for us, Harry analyzed our every move, and hanging out with the two of them pushed me to use my brains and make it through high school while avoiding the fact that I was attracted to guys, something I continued to hide for another dozen years.

"How are you guys doing? Brandon coming home for the holidays?"

Harry had adopted his wife's son when they married, and he was almost as gifted at electronic tinkering as Harry was, and had followed in Harry's footsteps to MIT.

"He's coming back this weekend. With something big to tell us. No idea what that is."

"Is he doing okay in school?"

"Yeah, yeah. A's and B's. I tell him not to worry, nobody's going to ask for his grades after he graduates. As long as he has that degree."

I brought up the last time I had seen Brandon, shortly before he left for his freshman year. I hadn't gotten any gaydar from him; he was one hundred percent geek.

Not to say you can't be a gay geek; I'd met a few of them in my time. But my niece Alina is his age, and they were often thrown together at parties. They'd been good pals when they were younger, but as she blossomed he seemed to shrink into his shell around her.

Yeah, whatever announcement Brandon had, it wasn't going to be coming out.

"What's the reason for the call?" Harry asked. "Holiday wishes?"

"Actually, can you check the surf report for me at Koko Head and Makapu'u Point, for yesterday morning? Any mention of a rip tide?"

"This a police investigation?" Harry asked, as I heard his fingers tapping in the background.

"Missing persons. Mother and son vacationers from New Orleans."

"Ouch. How old?"

"The boy is fourteen. No idea if he or the mother are strong swimmers."

"Here we go," he said. "No reports yesterday of any dangerous currents. Little wind, surf conditions only mediocre."

I thanked him, told him to keep in touch. "I want to hear what Brandon's secret announcement is. If you can share it."

"I will keep you in the loop."

Eventually I reached Koko Head. I cruised slowly through the parking lot there, and at Hanauma Bay Park next door, for Karen

Fontenot's rental car. Even though I didn't see it, I showed the pictures of her and Charles to the guards at both places. No one recognized either mother or son.

I repeated the process at Koko Head Botanical Garden and all the way up to the Hawai'i Kai golf course. No luck anywhere.

Chapter 5
On the Trail

I checked in at lunch with Queen Jones, the sergeant from the traffic department who was coordinating the searchers. No one had found anything yet. Then, following Terri's suggestion, I went all the way back on the Kalaniana'ole Freeway to Laukahi Street, a twisty road full of switchbacks that climbed up in the mountains. At the end of Okoa Street, I found the start of the Wiliwilinui Ridge Trail.

The trailhead was inside a gated community, Waialae Iki. If you wanted to hike, you had to check in at the guard house where the guard would write down your license plate number and give you a parking pass.

"No cars overnight," he said. "We don't allow that." Even so, I checked his list from the day before, and showed him the pictures of Karen and Charles Fontenot. It wasn't a surprise that he didn't recognize them.

Because I don't like to answer my personal cell while driving, particularly during a work day, when I checked the phone before leaving Waialae Iki, I noticed a couple of missed calls and text messages from my eldest brother, Lui, the station manager for KVOL,

Honolulu's scrappy independent station. He had heard there were missing tourists, and wanted any insight I had.

I texted back that the Media and Public Relations department at Honolulu PD would be able to answer any of his questions, and added a smiley emoticon at the end, just because it was the way we went back and forth when he needed police information.

I checked a number of other trailheads and parking lots, working my way back to headquarters, without any result. Queen Jones had taken over our squad room as her home base. She had the stocky build of her namesake, Queen Lili'uokalani, with the same kind of regal grace. I could easily see her in a tiara and a ball gown, though I was sure she'd hate it.

She handed me a new bulletin. "The family gave us mistaken information. They rented two cars when they arrived at the airport, one in Karen's name, the other in her brother Jules's name. When Karen left yesterday morning, she took Jules's car."

"And they just figured this out now?"

She shrugged. "The mother, Belle, had booked a Pearl Harbor tour for this afternoon. When they went to leave, that's when they realized which car she had taken."

"Hold on. Their daughter, sister, nephew, grandson, are missing, and they're going sightseeing?"

"I don't know what to tell you, Kimo. Except that we've been wasting our time looking for the wrong car all day."

"I showed pictures everywhere I went. I know they weren't seen anywhere."

Ray arrived a few minutes later. Sampson was in his office, and the two of us walked over there and rapped lightly on the door frame. Just like old times, when we needed his attention.

"Raymond Donne," he said, standing up and extending his hand. "Good to see you back here."

They shook hands, and Ray walked into Sampson's office and took a seat. "You might as well come in, too, Kimo," Sampson said.

He turned to Ray. "You've heard about the missing mother and son?"

Ray nodded. "I did a lot of study and work during these last few years with special needs kids," Ray said. "I understand the kid in this case has Oppositional Defiant Disorder."

"How do you know that?"

"I read it in the *Star-Advertiser* this morning," he said. "We had a program in the township where I worked. We invited anyone with special needs teenagers to come into the station and introduce themselves. I personally trained all the beat cops how to recognize a kid like that, who might appear shifty or otherwise guilty simply because he wouldn't look an officer in the face, kept his hands hidden, that kind of thing."

Sampson nodded approvingly, as officers and detectives started coming in from their search.

"I'm saying he, because most of the kids in that position are male. There are the occasional females, but many of the behaviors are the same."

"What do you do when one of these kids won't talk to you?" Sampson asked.

"Food. Especially if you can find out from the parents what the kid's favorite food is. Food is a great motivator." He leaned forward. "It's also important to know what the kid is intrigued by. A lot of kids on the autism spectrum are very smart, and obsessively interested in certain things, like dinosaurs or trains. If you know that, you can often get them started talking about what they care about."

"You two always made a good team," Sampson said. He steepled his hands and thought for a moment.

"No one in any position of power is happy about the Fontenots being missing," he said. "But the mayor is worried about the optics of this case. Devoted mother, avid hiker, neurodivergent son. And by the way, language is going to be very important in any statements we make. We're not doctors or psychiatrists, but we are smart enough to avoid words like retarded, abnormal, weird or psychotic."

"Of course," I said, and Ray nodded.

"It shouldn't come as a surprise to you that a lot of officials hope that what happens to these people can be shown to be an accident. Or worst case, that it was a family dispute that has no negative implications for tourism, or for the safety of our parks and natural features."

He stared across the room for a moment. "Right now we have over one hundred missing persons across the state. Some of those, we assume, are mentally ill or substance abusers who have deliberately walked away from their families. Others are people who met with misadventure—fell off a sailboat, for example. Another group are homicide victims whose bodies we have not found yet."

I wondered where this was going.

"There are those in government and tourism who are worried that some of those homicide victims are the work of a serial killer."

"Another Honolulu Strangler?" I asked. "Wouldn't we already have ideas about that?"

"Apparently an article is circulating about how many people are missing in American national parks," Sampson said. "It has been suggested, and I can't say by whom or in what context, that we need to actively pursue all missing persons in the context of the Fontenot case."

Ray nodded. "In case this is not a domestic problem but someone out there stalking natural areas looking for victims and either burying them or leaving their bodies in inaccessible places."

"I knew you were good for something, Donne," Sampson said, smiling.

He pursed his lips again, and we waited.

"Here's what I'm thinking. I can use the fear circulating through city government to authorize the additional detective position I've been lobbying for."

We waited.

"I'm going to need information from you before I can push your hiring. I want to know everything you've done that involves kids, particularly neurodiverse ones. Can you get that to me by tomorrow morning?"

"How detailed do you want it?"

"Nothing that would compromise the integrity of a case, of course. But any classes you've taken, including the curriculum if you can get it. Any examples of your ability to deal with kids like Charles Fontenot, including all the work you did in training other cops."

"I can do that."

Sampson stood up. "Then I'll do my best to get a special exemption hire moving forward. It may be next week, or the week after. But obviously the mayor's office thinks this has a high priority, so I'm hoping sooner rather than later."

"Thanks, Lieutenant. I enjoyed the years that I worked in your command, and coming back is the best career move I can hope for."

"Then let's go see what's on the news," Sampson said.

We walked back into the staff room in time for the four o'clock news on KVOL. I watched the lava flow at the beginning of the credits, with the voice over "KVOL: Exploding News all the Time."

The lead story was about the missing Fontenots. Ralph Kim, a reporter I'd tangled with in the past, was on site in front of the Albergo d'Italia in Kahala. He was a handsome guy, and always dressed impeccably in sharp suits with perfect hair, but there was something smarmy about him I'd hated for years, ever since he had a part in my very public coming out.

Queen and a couple of the other detectives and officers joined us as we watched a TV mounted on the wall. "Fear is rising here in Kahala for the fate of a mother and son who went hiking yesterday morning in the mountains around Honolulu and who have not yet returned," Ralph said, in his best broadcaster voice.

Someone back at the station brought up photos of Karen and Charles. They were both grinning, but Karen's smile seemed tired, maybe even forced. I was sure that raising a neurodiverse kid like Charles couldn't have been easy.

"Both mother and son are experienced hikers, but as we locals know, our mountains can be deceptively dangerous," Ralph continued. "And the possibility exists that they could have met up with misfortune." He looked grave, as if he was already planning to speak at their funerals. He ended with a plea for anyone with information to call KVOL's 24-hour news hotline.

Then the broadcast shifted to Honolulu Hale, the seat of city government. It was a white stucco building with red tile roofs, surrounded by tall palm trees. The mayor spoke outside, in front of large inflatable statues of Santa Claus and his wife. He reassured the citizens that HPD was on the case and there was no need to worry, and encouraged people to call our tip line if they spotted either Charles or Karen.

The rest of the team straggled in as the news shifted to an accident on the H-1 highway. I could see the long shift wearing on many of our people, some of whom had worked the night shift before being called in this morning.

Sampson made the announcement about the wrong car, and people groaned. "It's probably not news to you, but we've gotten a very tepid response from community members we have asked for help finding the Fontenots."

"People I spoke to said that we can't be responsible for every tourist who gets lost," Steve Hart said, and I wondered how many people he'd actually spoken with.

But Mary Luo seconded his opinion. "I called a lot of folks I know in Chinatown to recruit volunteers, and no one said yes."

"It's an example of how divided this country has become," Steve said. "Three, four years ago, we would have seen the colleges, the churches, the citizens' groups, all turning out to search. Today, they don't care."

I had to agree with him. Because of my close connection to Sandra, people loved to talk to me about politics and how screwed up the country had become.

"The good news is that we've been getting tips on the hot line,"

Sampson said. "I'm looking for volunteers to stick around for a few more hours and follow them up."

Only a handful of staffers volunteered. Grudgingly, I raised my hand too. I'd gotten a good night's sleep, unlike many of my colleagues, and I didn't have a family to rush home to, just a partner and a dog, who could fend for themselves for a few more hours.

As I sat at my desk to begin following up on tips, my cell phone rang again. Lui.

This time I answered. "What's the matter, brah, not happy with the information gathering from your stellar reporter Mr. Kim? You've got to track down sources yourself?"

"Sources, as you call them, indicate this boy is dangerous," my brother said. "If he is, you owe it to the people of Hawai'i to let them know so they can take precautions."

"Lui. We're talking about a fourteen-year-old boy and his mother, out hiking. He doesn't have an assault rifle and he's not a danger to the general population."

"Can I quote you on that?"

"Of course not. You know all official information has to come from the department."

"But you've got to give me something, brah," he said. "Remember, I changed your diapers."

"You say that, but Mom disagrees," I said. "But if you did, I hope I peed on you."

"Kimo."

"Look, all I can say is that we've got officers and detectives out checking every trailhead. We are doing our best to find this woman and her son." Then I lowered my voice. "Although it's weird that they gave us the wrong license plate number for the car she took. And the family doesn't seem that concerned."

"I get that, too," he said. "They wouldn't even talk to Ralph directly, and we had to dig up that photo on our own."

"It could be that they're private people," I said. "But there's something odd about that family. I can't put my finger on it yet. But it's something you could follow up on."

He thanked me and hung up. I spent the next two hours at my desk, with a list of callers who had said they had seen either Karen or Charles Fontenot or had their own ideas about what might have happened. One woman was convinced that someone crazy who lived up in the crevices of the Ko'olau was killing hikers, though she had no concrete evidence.

Another thought she saw Karen at the Foodland Farms in Aina Hana, wearing a blonde wig and big sunglasses. "Was her son with her?" I asked.

"No, she was with a big Samoan man. Do you think he was keeping her son locked up somewhere?"

"To force her to go grocery shopping with him?" I asked.

There must have been something snarky in my tone, because she hung up.

A man who had been at the Ala Wai Marina that morning had seen a woman and boy of about the right age board a charter fishing boat, but when I tracked down the captain he verified that the people he had taken were not the Fontenots.

I worked through my list and then drove home, so tired that my eyes kept closing on the H2. I managed to stay awake until I got to Aiea Heights, though, and fortunately Mike had saved me a half a pizza. He heated it up for me while I drank a couple of big glasses of water.

Mike and I talked briefly, but I kept yawning and by ten o'clock I was zonked out. My last thoughts were of Karen and Charles Fontenot, and I hoped they were sleeping safely somewhere. Though I doubted it.

Chapter 6
Big News

By the time I woke up Wednesday morning the story had exploded. Mike and I ate breakfast in the kitchen with the TV on. Not usual for us; we both liked to start the morning in a more mellow way, and we'd even begun doing yoga together or meditating briefly.

But I was curious to know if Karen or Charles had come back, so I turned on Wake Up, Honolulu!, KVOL's morning program. They led, as always, with a report on the weather and surf conditions on the North Shore, but quickly segued into a follow-up to the Fontenot disappearance.

After a brief recap, the co-host, Maile Gomes, a perky young Hawaiian woman with lush dark hair who liked to wear pink orchid leis on camera, informed us solemnly that Karen and Charles were still missing. "Our first guest this morning is going to fill us in on how dangerous this young man might be," she said. She looked straight at the camera. "Which the police haven't revealed officially yet."

They'd brought on a local child psychologist named Dr. Eileen Matluck, who was introduced as having lots of experience with developmentally delayed children. "What can you tell us about Charles Fontenot?" Maile asked.

"As a boy, he was diagnosed with Asperger's Syndrome," Dr. Matluck said. "Because of this Charles is likely to have significant difficulties in social interaction and nonverbal communication, along with restricted and repetitive patterns of behavior and interests."

"Does he bang his head against the wall?" Maile asked, looking concerned.

"I can't say for certain, but it's more likely that he exhibits behavior like repeatedly washing his hands or nodding his head."

"Are they allowed to put all this stuff on TV?" Mike asked me. "This is a fourteen-year-old boy. Aren't there privacy issues around revealing his mental health details?"

"This is KVOL we're talking about. Broadcast first, get permission later."

Mike frowned, but we both kept watching, as if we were seeing a train wreck unfolding in front of us. Which perhaps we were.

"You said there's something else wrong with him, though," Maile said.

"Yes, he's also been diagnosed with Oppositional Defiant Disorder," Dr. Matluck said. "Children with ODD are uncooperative, defiant, and hostile toward peers, parents, teachers, and other authority figures. He's likely to be angry and perhaps violent, especially if he's outside his normal routine."

"Like being out in the mountains," Maile said, looking concerned.

"He's normally home-schooled in New Orleans, with minimal exposure to the outside world. I'd say this whole family vacation could be one big trigger."

Maile faced the camera again. "Karen and Charles traveled here from their home in New Orleans with Karen's mother, her two brothers and other family members. And yet the family has been curiously unconcerned about Karen's and Charles's whereabouts. They weren't even reported missing until a day after they disappeared, and it appears the family gave the police misleading evidence."

"Really?" Mike asked.

I told him about the different license plates. "Could be a simple human error," I said. "Or it could be something more."

Maile thanked Dr. Matluck and promised further updates during the day, then transitioned to a segment on the triumphant return of a family's lost turtle.

At the morning briefing, Queen announced that we were expanding the search to head farther toward the Leeward Coast, and I was assigned to check out the parking lots and trailheads I hadn't hit the day before.

It was nearly eleven o'clock by the time I reached the Wa'ahila Ridge trailhead. I knew the park well, because while I was growing up my parents lived in St. Louis Heights, and our house backed up on one of the park's wooded fingers. I wound my way up St. Louis Road, turning right on Peter St. near the top. At the cul-de-sac at the end of Peter I turned onto Ruth Street, a tiny road that led me to the parking lot.

Several streets there bore first names—besides Peter and Ruth, there were Saul and Noah, Felix and Robert. Growing up my friends and I had imagined that they were kids like us, wondering if someday we'd have streets named for us. It was only later, while I was investigating a case, that I learned there was a Kimo Street in Waianae on the Leeward Coast

It was a hot, sunny day and I hoped that Karen and Charles, if they were still alive and lost somewhere, had ample shade and water. I was going through the motions of checking the license plate numbers of the cars parked at Wa'ahila Ridge when I found the match. It surprised me, and I read the plate number twice before I called Queen.

I gave her the directions to the parking lot, and she promised to send uniforms to close off the street and start calling searchers in from other places to join me. "I'll head into the forest," I said. "I know this area pretty well."

"Be careful, Kimo. According to his family Charles could be

angry and defiant. There's a strong possibility that Charles hurt his mother and he could be dangerous."

"Yeah, I heard that on KVOL this morning. Interesting that they had that news before we did."

"We're busy looking for this mother and son. They've got their resources allocated differently. What can they dig up to make the headlines more scandalous?"

I agreed with that. Before I left my SUV, I made sure I had a bottle of water, my gun and a canister of pepper spray. I was taking Queen's advice to heart. From a box in the back of the SUV I also pulled a roll of crime scene tape and a long hank of pink ribbon left over from the twins' last birthday. I picked up a copy of the area map from a box at the start of the trail.

I began climbing the footpath, moving slowly, looking to my right and left for any disturbed foliage that might indicate someone had passed before me. It was cool and quiet up there, only the occasional rustle of wind in the ironwoods and the call of a bird.

After a half hour of climbing, I hadn't met another soul on the path, but I came to a spot that looked disturbed. It appeared that some branches of an ironwood had been split off by a lightning strike, and they formed a leafy canopy to my right. I edged in slowly, careful not to disturb anything, and saw that a number of the branches had fallen off.

The canopy blocked my view to the right, and I stepped closer. It was only because I was moving so slowly and carefully that I didn't slide down the slope which appeared almost by magic as I pushed aside the last hanging branch.

I made sure I had my balance before looking down. A woman's body rested at the bottom of a steep ravine, and it matched Karen Fontenot's description, down to the bright yellow hiking boots she had brought with her to Honolulu, which were missing from her room.

I stepped carefully back to the trail. There was no cell phone signal there, but before I moved back down the hillside toward the parking lot, I blocked off the entrance to the canopied area with crime scene tape.

Then every six feet as I moved down the trail, I cut off a piece of pink ribbon and marked a tree branch. I wasn't going to depend on breadcrumbs to find my way back.

Chapter 7
Venom

As soon as I could get a bar on my cell phone, I started trying to call Queen. I was almost back to the parking lot before I reached her. "I spotted the body of a woman matching Ms. Fontenot's description," I said, struggling to keep my voice calm after the exertion of hiking and the adrenaline shock of finding the body.

"Any sign of the boy?"

"No. Do you want me to wait here for backup or head up the trail again?" I told her how I had marked the location, and how steep the slope had been where Karen had fallen.

"Stay there. Does it look like a team will be able to get the body up that hill or will they need to look for a different way in?"

"It's pretty steep. I could try and find another way but I don't want to disturb the area any more than I already have, in case there's something down there that will lead us to Charles."

"Roger that. I should have the first uniforms there in minutes."

She was as good as her word about sending uniforms, and within minutes I saw the whirling lights of an approaching marked car.

The next hour moved very quickly. Uniforms and other department personnel fanned out through the woods, finding hikers in the park and escorting them down, and then closing off the parking lot.

Crime scene techs arrived; one team checked the car, while I led the other up the trail and pointed through the canopy.

The lead tech, Larry Solas, backed away carefully. "I can see the way she slid down there. Way too steep for us to approach without help from the SWAT team. They're trained to rappel."

While Larry and another tech took samples from under the canopy, I went back down to the trailhead and tried to beat my own path to the bottom of the ravine. I was hot and sweaty and I couldn't make much progress. Branches slapped and scratched me, bugs swarmed wherever my skin was exposed, and I gave up after about half an hour.

If Charles Fontenot had made it down that slope and then somewhere else, I wasn't going to find him going in the way I had.

By the time I returned to the canopy area, a couple of SWAT officers were there, setting up a rappel line to get down to the bottom of the ravine. I wanted to go down, too, but one of them, a guy named Dennis Opaka, had been cross-trained in evidence collection, and he was going to check the area once the body was removed.

I lingered there. I could have helped explore the area and look for Charles, but I felt a duty, as the person who had found her, to stay as close as I could to Karen Fontenot.

Eventually a helicopter arrived and lowered a pallet down to the ground to lift her body out of the ravine. I watched the whole operation, and then helped Larry and his team ferry collection kits back down to the parking lot.

It was dusk by then, and the department declared it was too dangerous to keep searching through the park, with its twisty paths and deadly slopes. We were dismissed, to reconvene at the trailhead the next morning to continue the search for Charles.

As I was preparing to leave, Sampson called my cell. "Two things," he said. "First, you're getting your partner back tomorrow morning. He's only a temporary hire, while they process all the paperwork, but I'm confident he'll be with us long-term." He paused. "I need to ask you a favor. Since you're the one who found the body, can you go out to Kahala and talk to the family? A liaison officer has already broken the news to them, but they are understandably worried and want to know as much as they can."

"What can I say about the boy?" I asked. "I'm sure they're going to ask. But there was no trace of him anywhere near his mother."

"I have faith in you. You'll figure it out. I've got to go," he said. "Press conference. Talk to you tomorrow."

Then the line was dead.

I got into my SUV. At least I'd have my work husband back the next day; that was great news.

It was funny; for years Mike had called Ray my work husband, occasionally complaining that I spent more time with Ray than with him. Then a year ago he'd gained his own work wife—an assistant fire chief who worked under him. The balance had shifted then, and I was the one complaining. Well, all that was about to change.

I kept seeing flashes of Karen Fontenot's body splayed out at the bottom of the ravine as I drove down to the Albergo d'Italia. I showed my badge to the desk clerk and asked for the Fontenots' room numbers, and then asked if there was somewhere I could freshen up before seeing them. My face and hands were dirty and scratched up by the branches in the park, and I could smell my dried sweat.

He directed me to a men's room that was lavishly appointed in marble and gold fixtures. I felt like a slummer in there as I pulled off my shirt, washed my face and arms, and applied a deodorant stick. Then I donned a clean aloha shirt I kept in the car for this very purpose. I dropped the dirty shirt back at the SUV and then went up to the first of the two rooms I'd been given.

No answer, so I tried the second. The bloated man who answered the door was in his fifties, and he sneered at me. Before I had a chance to pull my badge out and introduce myself, he said, "We didn't call for room service," and closed the door.

Sure, I was wearing an aloha shirt, but I didn't have one of those oval badges with my name on it. Give me a break.

I knocked again, this time with my badge in my hand. "Detective Kanapa'aka, HPD," I said. "I'm here to talk to Ms. Fontenot's family."

"Let him in, Jules." The voice that floated out towards us was old and querulous. "I'm not getting any younger."

I stepped into a suite with a large living room that looked out at the Pacific, now a deadly dark mass. The elderly woman who spoke sat in an armchair, holding a cane in her right hand. "I am Belle Fontenot. Karen is my daughter."

She spoke with only the barest hint of a southern accent. She had the same kind of aristocratic grace I'd seen in Terri's parents, born of wealth and educated in private schools.

"You met my oldest son, Jules," she said, nodding toward him.

Jules Fontenot had none of his mother's aristocratic grace. Despite his expensive clothes and gold jewelry, he had the air of a bully. And that wasn't just because he had been rude to me at the door.

Jules took over the introductions then. "My wife, Emeline," he said, motioning to a slim well-dressed woman with the kind of smoothly pulled skin that results from facial surgery. She sat across from her mother-in-law, with an expression of distaste on her face, as if she'd been drawn into someone else's drama and knew she didn't belong there.

I nodded to her, and she inclined her head slightly.

"And my brother Leo," Jules continued, motioning to another man in his fifties with sallow skin and messy hair. Curiously he wore a long-sleeved shirt, and I wondered if the air conditioning was set too high for him. He didn't acknowledge me at all.

"My daughter and son are here in Hawaii with us but they are out somewhere in the hotel now," Jules continued. "What have you come here to tell us?"

No one asked me to take a seat, so I stood there while Jules Fontenot poured himself and his wife a pair of glasses of scotch from an expensive bottle that they must have bought in the hotel gift shop.

"I grew up in the woods where I found your daughter's body," I said carefully. "My boss asked me to come over and fill in some details."

"Yes, go on," Belle said.

"Just off the trail, about a half hour in from the parking lot, an ironwood tree fell in a lightning strike. The fallen branches obscured the fact that there is a very slippery and steep slope off to the right."

I felt the need to explain. "Ironwood looks like a weeping willow, with that kind of leaves." Belle and Emeline nodded in recognition.

"We had to bring in a SWAT team to rappel down the slope and then a helicopter to airlift Ms. Fontenot out. The Medical Examiner will examine her and we hope that tomorrow we'll have a cause of death."

"What about the boy?" Belle asked.

"We haven't been able to locate him yet. The area your daughter chose to hike is posted as dangerous, and it's possible that he either fell somewhere nearby, in an attempt to reach his mother, or that he's wandering in the woods."

"He wouldn't go after her," Jules said. "He hated her."

"Jules!" Belle said sharply.

"It's the truth. He hated everyone. Each of us. The staff at Terre Riche. Every teacher and every student at every school he ever attended."

The other man, Leo, said, "My brother is trying to say that Charles's medical condition made him a difficult person to get along with. I'm not sure he is capable of caring, or love."

I turned to him. "Does he have any wilderness survival skills?"

He laughed. "He has a knack for survival, I'll give him that. Any other kid with his problems would have been beaten to a pulp by other kids or locked up in an institution."

"Leo, that's enough," Belle said. "The boy is our blood and he is missing. Have some respect."

"What I believe my brother is trying to communicate," Jules began carefully. From his demeanor I imagined him speaking to a jury. "Is that you can't trust anything Charles says. Even if you find him and he tells you what he thinks happened, you can't believe it. He is like an angry balloon hovering over our family, filled with venom, that trickles out in small doses, falling on anyone who happens to be nearby. His mother was often the object of his rage. It would not surprise me, or any of us, to know that he pushed my sister down that hill."

"He might not have been trying to kill her," Emeline said, and because her lips hardly moved it took me a moment to realize she was speaking. "He often pushed her and hit her, but he always apologized later, and she moved on. I wouldn't tolerate that kind of behavior from my children, but I recognize a mother's love when I see it."

I spoke to the room at large. "Is there any possibility that Charles might be armed? I don't mean guns—does he carry a knife, for example?"

"He has a Swiss Army knife with all kinds of attachments," Leo said. "He uses it to cut leaves and branches. And he's obsessed with the fish scaler though I've never seen him actually use it on a fish."

I stood there for a moment longer, trying to avoid the rancor floating in the air. Though both the women had more generous feelings about Charles, the men were in opposition. Finally I said, "Is there anything else I can tell you?"

No one answered, so I sketched a short bow and turned toward the door.

"Thank you, detective," Belle said to my back.

I looked back over my shoulder. "I wish I had more information to give you." Then I walked out of the suite and closed the door carefully behind me. The simple hallway, lined with watercolors of Hawaiian scenes, welcomed me in a way I hadn't felt in the suite behind me.

Chapter 8
Lost Boy

The search for Charles Fontenot began in earnest Thursday morning. All available police department members were recruited to comb the ins and outs of the Wa'ahila Ridge Park. Before I left the house, I packed myself a quick bag—a clean shirt, boxers and slacks, a can of antiperspirant, a package of wipes and a few other things I thought might come in handy.

I strapped on a belly bag that Mike and I often used when hiking, with bug repellent, two bottles of water, and a couple of packages of cheese and crackers. I called Ray before I left. "You'll be at work this morning?"

"Probably not until noon. Meetings with HR, forms to fill out, videos to watch."

"Can't they hold that off? We've got a missing boy."

"The wheels of human resources grind very slowly," he said. "But they grind exceedingly fine."

"I believe the exact quote is something to do with the mills of the gods," I said. "But close enough. See you when I see you."

Queen led off our eight AM meeting with a chilling warning, which I'd already heard, though not in so much detail.

"Charles Fontenot has been diagnosed as being a high-functioning individual on the autism spectrum. He has undoubtedly been traumatized by the time he has been missing and may respond with violence to any physical overture. He may not respond appropriately to verbal commands. Personnel should proceed with extreme caution when approaching him, as he may be considered dangerous."

"I spoke with the family last night. Charles carries a Swiss Army knife with multiple blades, and he's accustomed to using it to cut leaves and branches," I said.

"Make that armed and dangerous," Queen said.

Now was when I really needed Ray by my side, with his experience with neurodiverse kids. But instead he was upstairs somewhere filling out forms and watching videos.

Queen went through all the assignments, and I volunteered to check the area behind the house where I'd grown up, because I knew it so well. As the rest of the team filtered away, I went up to Queen. "What are we supposed to do if we can't approach Charles and we can't talk to him? He sounds feral."

"Did you take that seminar on dealing with kids with developmental disabilities?" she asked.

I shook my head. "I tried. But I have two kids, and it just... I couldn't watch it."

"You need to. The material is really important. According to this one research report, people with disabilities, including those on the autism spectrum, are five times more likely to be incarcerated than people in the general population. Civilian injuries and fatalities during police interactions are disproportionately common."

I thought about Addie and Owen. So far, we had been incredibly lucky. They were growing up as intelligent, caring, responsible kids. We'd had our share of broken bones and stitches, but that was because they were learning to take calculated risks. A tree that was easy to climb, for example, was much more dangerous after a rainstorm when the branches were slippery.

I resolved that if I ran across him, I would treat Charles Fontenot with the same care I'd want for my own kids. "I'll rely on this handout," I said to Queen.

I read further as I walked toward my SUV. I learned that kids with autism may keep their hands in their pockets because it's a coping mechanism, not because they are holding a weapon.

They may repeat a word because it helps them focus.

They may refuse to make eye contact, seem fidgety, or appear prepared to run away.

At the end of the sheet there was some specific information about Charles Fontenot. "He has a fascination with trees, leaves, stones, and bugs," I read. "He may have accumulated a collection of these and he will be very protective of them. Calmly asking him questions about the items he is holding may allow him to feel comfortable enough to share what he knows. But be prepared for a fountain of knowledge!"

The final lines were the most chilling. "Charles is NOT stupid. His brain simply works in a different way from most people. In addition to his learning difficulties, he has been diagnosed with a persistent pattern of anger, irritability, arguing, defiance or vindictiveness toward parents and other authority figures. It is imperative not to attempt to treat him as a small child or establish a power imbalance."

I shook my head. Normal policing was all about the power imbalance. My badge immediately signified that I had the power to stop a suspect, question her, handcuff him, take them into the station for interrogation. Citizens who questioned that power politely received, in general, a polite response.

Violent resistance, however, led to violence in turn, though we had been trained for years to minimize that level of aggression through preventive measures.

How could you address that power differential with a kid whose brain was wired to reject it?

I drove back to Wa'ahila Ridge, but instead of crowding the parking lot, which I was sure was already filled with various police vehicles, I called Carolyn Lau. She was an accountant with the firm my father had used to handle his business, and I had met her and her husband a few times.

"Hey, Carolyn, it's Kimo Kanapa'aka. How's the house treating you?"

"Your father took good care of it," she said. "We had to replace the roof last year, but that's just normal wear and tear. What's up?"

"I don't know if you follow the news, but there's a lost teenaged boy and we think he might be on Wa'ahila Ridge," I said, avoiding the mention of his dead mother. "You think I could park in your driveway and get into the woods back there?"

"I read about that," she said. "An officer distributed a flyer to our house last night warning us about him. That he might have killed his mother, and that we should be very careful if we spotted him. Do you think he could be near us?"

"We have personnel combing the whole park," I said. "I simply thought I'd start behind your place because I know it so well."

"Of course. Eldon and I are both at work and the boys are in school, though. Will you need to get inside?"

"No, no, I just wanted to let you know I might be skulking around the area, and not to worry."

"I have three very active boys," Carolyn said. "Worry is my middle name. Do whatever you need to help find this one."

I thanked her and promised to be gone by the time she and her family got home.

It was a weird trip back in time for me, pulling up in front of a house that had once been my home. The landscaping around the front was different, and the house had been painted a darker shade of beige. A couple of bikes were parked along the side of the house, which my father would never have allowed. Bikes belonged in the garage, hanging on hooks, when they were not being ridden.

When I was a kid, there was no clear line between where our property ended and the park began. The grass toward the back was overgrown, with saplings springing up, and so there was a transition zone between civilization and wilderness.

Unruly Son

Eldon Lau had a different idea. Now, the manicured lawn stopped at a wooden fence, which kept out the encroachment of the wild. I pulled the latch and opened the gate in the center of the fence, and stepped almost immediately into Narnia.

Trees and brush clustered up at the back of the wall, though there was a narrow trail, obviously created by the Lau boys, that led into the woods. I followed it until it petered out after about twenty feet, in a very small clearing where I could see remnants of a wooden fort the boys might have built.

I examined the area very carefully, because it seemed like the kind of place Charles Fontenot might have discovered and used for shelter. But there was no evidence that anyone had been back there in weeks—weeds grew up unhindered in the dirt floor, and nothing in the area looked like it had been disturbed.

It was so quiet back there, sheltered from the noise of cars pushing up against the twists and turns of St. Louis Drive. Somehow the woods seemed kinder there than the area where I'd found Karen Fontenot's body. There were no steep slides, just a gradual climb, and no damaged trees either.

For the next couple of hours, I was a boy again, exploring the woods. I forgot about my responsibilities, even about Charles Fontenot, and focused on covering every inch of my territory. I was Kamehameha the Great, having sailed my outrigger to this new island and seeking to bring it under my dominion. I was Peter Pevensie, exploring the land on the other side of the wardrobe.

That's where my imagination ran as a kid, and I let it go that day, trying to see the forest as a fourteen-year-old might. The word "ko'olau" means windward, and because these mountains faced the wind, they trapped precipitation, which resulted in numerous streams and waterfalls.

If I were alone in the park, I'd need water to survive. Charles, with his regular pattern of hikes with his mother, would know that too. I listened closely as I climbed, and eventually heard the sound of running water. It was faint and first and then louder, as I got closer.

I could see no signs that a human had gone near, or into, the water, so I kept climbing. I recognized a few patches of edible mushrooms and berries in the woods, but I didn't see any indication that someone had picked through them.

I climbed and climbed, following the stream uphill, but found no sign of Charles. When I reached the waterfall at the very top, I stopped to drink from the cool water, and eat my cheese and crackers. Then I carefully picked my way across the stream and started downhill again.

Despite the fact that there were searchers throughout the park, I didn't see another soul until I finally descended to the parking lot in the late afternoon. My face was scratched, my shirt was streaked with sweat, and I itched from bug bites on my arms and legs.

I was standing with Mary Luo, who looked as miserable as I felt, when her radio crackled. "All units, forecast is for rainstorms in the Ko'olaus this evening, so search is suspended for today. All units return to base for recap meeting."

"I don't like the idea of that kid being out in the woods if storms are coming in," Mary said.

"I don't either, but everything we've heard says that he's smart and an experienced hiker. He'll find himself shelter."

"It's what we all have to believe, isn't it?" Mary asked.

Chapter 9
Wrong Move

My brother Lui lived only a few streets away from where I had parked, so I called my sister-in-law Liliha. "Hey, are you home?" I asked. "I'm a couple of blocks away and I wanted to stop by."

"I'm here. What's up?"

I talked as I drove, explaining about the search for Charles Fontenot. "I could use a quick shower and a place to change my clothes. And you don't happen to have any aloe, do you?"

"I have a huge plant at the edge of the patio. I'll break off a stem for you."

Aloe was our family remedy for bug bites, scalded fingers, and minor scratches long before the rest of the world caught onto its medicinal properties. When I walked up to Liliha's door carrying my bag, she was waiting for me.

"Your skin doesn't look good," she said, handing me the spiky stem.

"I'll be fine."

"Spoken like every one of the Kanapa'aka boys. Do you know once Keoni got into a fight at school and the first thing he said to me was, 'don't worry, mama, this isn't my blood.'"

I laughed. "Smart kid."

I knew my way to the guest bathroom, where I stripped down, showered, and then liberally brushed the gooey end of the aloe stem over my bites and scratches. By the time I had sprayed myself and dressed again, I felt like a new man.

At least a somewhat bruised and battered version of a new man.

As I came out of the bathroom, my cell phone rang. Liliha must have told Lui I was at their house. "Hey, brah, understand you're enjoying my hospitality."

I wanted to say something snarky, but I bit my tongue. "Yup, I appreciate it."

"So what's new in this hunt for the boy?"

"Lui. You know I can't say anything more than the police line. We're still looking."

"One of my reporters heard something," he said. "About other people missing in state parks. Can you verify that?"

"It's public knowledge. Most of those people either wanted to drop off the map, or they're hiding from the law, or, in a very few cases, they met with an unfortunate end."

"So you're saying someone is out there killing people in the parks."

"That is not what I'm saying. You grew up in the mountains as much as I did. You know how easy it is to fall, to drown. One wrong move and you're history."

"Is that what happened to Karen Fontenot? She made a wrong move?"

"There's no report yet on what caused her death. You'd have to get that from the Medical Examiner's office."

"But there is a possibility that someone killed her, right? And that maybe that person has killed other people in the park?"

"You should have been a fiction writer, Lui. You come up with incredible stories."

"And that's what plays well at KVOL," he said. "Thanks, brah. Take care."

After he hung up I thought about what I'd said. Had I implied there was a serial killer out there? No. But maybe I hadn't been strong enough in arguing against the idea.

I gave up worrying. Lui would do whatever he thought would get ratings. I found Liliha in the living room, where she nodded approvingly at my transformation.

I kissed her cheek and thanked her for the hospitality and the aloe. "How's Malia doing at Pepperdine?" I asked. Her oldest, Jeffrey, had graduated from Harvard as his father wished, and worked at Bankoh doing something with international accounts. The middle boy, Keoni, defied his parents' expectations, majored in agriculture at UH, and had gone to work for my brother Haoa's landscaping firm, which he was whipping into shape after years of my brother's laid-back management style.

"I think she's majoring in fashion and makeup," Liliha said. "At least that's what I get from spying on her social media accounts. She never says anything about classes or projects. And it's costing us over $50,000 a year."

"You never know, she could become an influencer like the Kardashians," I said. "Isn't one of them the youngest female billionaire?"

"Your mouth to God's ear," she said, as I walked down the driveway to my SUV.

I wasn't the last person to straggle into the follow-up meeting, but I was certainly the freshest. "What did you do?" Mary Luo whispered to me as I slid into a chair beside her. Her straight black hair had puffed up in the humidity and there was a spot of dirt beneath her left ear.

"Snuck in a quick shower. If they want us to follow up on more phone leads, I figured I'd be here for a while."

But it appeared that once Karen's body had been found, the calls to the tip line had dried up. There were only a few dozen to follow up on, and they were shifted to District 6.

The meeting was short, since there wasn't much to share, and after it was finished I went back to my desk and called Ray. "What happened with HR?"

"Took longer than I thought. But the good news is that I'm starting tomorrow."

"Excellent. And how's the cabana house?"

"Great. A little small, but it'll do for us until we find something. We decided not to register Vinnie for school until we know what district we'll be in, so he's been happy as a clam swimming in the pool all day. Your kids are jealous."

"But they're getting along?"

"Oh, yeah. You know how plastic kids are at that age. Vinnie remembers them from before we left, and vice versa, and it's like they just picked up again."

I heard him speaking to someone in the background, and then he was back to me. "Julie and Cathy have been talking, and they want to invite you and Mike over for dinner. You think you can make six o'clock?"

I had long since learned my lesson about accepting invitations. "I'll check with Mike and text you." I called Mike's cell and left a message, then struck out for home.

I recognized his truck, with the red and yellow flames along the side, a few cars ahead of me, so I trailed him up Aiea Heights Drive and into our driveway.

"Hey," he said, as we both got out. "I thought you'd still be looking for that missing kid."

"Bad weather forecast, so they called the search. I feel bad, thinking the kid is out there in a storm, but Mary Luo reminded me he's an experienced hiker. So even if his brain works a little different from the rest of us, he's smart enough to find shelter."

We closed the distance between us and kissed hello, as Roby started barking from inside the house. "That dog is such a cock blocker," I said, as we backed apart.

"We can lock him out of the bedroom later if you want," Mike said with a grin.

Unruly Son

"Oh, about later. Did you get my message?"

Mike was happy not to have to cook or clean up, so I texted Ray a thumbs-up about dinner.

Chapter 10
Ohana

Mike and I finished our beers and walked farther up Aiea Heights Drive to the house Sandra and Cathy had bought after the twins were born. They'd been living in a waterfront condo close to downtown, and they'd wanted to be closer to us, and to give the kids a big house.

As we approached with Roby on a leash, we heard the sounds of screaming and squealing coming from the pool, and I opened the gate to the back yard and let him off his leash. A moment later I heard him cannonballing into the water with his human siblings.

We rounded the corner to see Ray at the backyard barbecue, which was usually Mike's domain, the three kids in the pool with Roby, and Cathy and Julie setting food onto a long picnic table.

Ray looked much as he had the last time I'd seen him, a year and a half before. Same sandy brown hair, trim physique, a couple of inches shorter than I was. He had a way of moving, commanding his physical space, and I was pleased to see that hadn't changed as he and I embraced.

"It is so good to see you," I said, when we pulled back. "Mike always called you my work husband and I didn't realize how much I would miss you until you were gone."

"Julie said the same thing about you."

I noticed the three kids racing around the wet edge of the pool. "Yo! Addie and Owen. You know better than to run where it's wet. Show some smarts and concern for your guest."

Ray laughed. "I think you yell at those kids for everything you must have done as a kid."

"I admit, I'm probably the most nervous parent among the four of us. How can you not be, seeing all the terrible things we see people do? Mike drills them on fire safety while Sandra is most concerned with things like not eating their toys. Cathy is the most laissez-faire of all of us. She believes that kids are strong and resilient and need the chance to explore the world and learn their own lessons."

Ray nodded. "I wouldn't disagree with that."

"You know, she started feeding them interesting adult food as soon as they moved on from liquids and mush. Sometimes they surprise me with their sophisticated international palates. They know their favorite types of sushi, of falafel, of burritos. They both love salt bagels with cream cheese, lox and capers, which don't correspond to any of our gene pools."

"Vinnie isn't that adventurous when it comes to food. Chicken fingers, spaghetti and tomato sauce, hamburgers and peanut butter and jelly sandwiches. Maybe he'll open up around them."

I turned to him. "Don't you worry about him, though? Sometimes I lay awake at night and I can't fall asleep. One wrong decision—taking a pill someone gave them, driving with someone intoxicated, miscalculating a leap into a swimming pool—and they could be killed, or have their lives unalterably changed."

"It's true," Ray said. Becoming a father is the most frightening thing that's ever happened to me. But it's the most amazing thing, too. You can't let the fear overwhelm the joy."

"I know." I rested my arm on the back of an Adirondack chair painted bright yellow. "But then I think about Charles Fontenot, and how he's turned out. That makes me remember how a Punahou friend's son developed schizophrenia at sixteen, with no family history. A kid who lived down the street from us jumped from a highway bridge at eighteen after a girl broke up with him. I could go on and on."

"I'm sure you could. And I'm sure I'll hear more about this at work. But right now, let's try and enjoy the evening, all right?"

"I'll try," I said.

"Good to see your sense of knowing just the right thing to say is still intact."

Ray had to get back to the burgers, which needed flipping, and Mike moved in to help. I went over to say hi to Julie, to hug her and welcome her back, too. "I'm sorry things didn't work out in Philadelphia, but I'm really glad you guys are here again."

She had always been a sweet-natured woman, the balance to Ray's tough guy, but the year and a half away had brought out some new lines in her forehead and a few strands of gray in her hair. She looked like she could use a few days relaxing by the pool.

"Turns out all this sunshine can spoil a gal," she said. "Both of us had forgotten how much we hate snow. My job was all numbers, all the time, and I hated it." She leaned in close. "Ray won't say anything, but he couldn't settle in at his job, either. He learned something about dealing with people out here, and when he tried to bring that back, he got shot down. You wouldn't believe some of things he told me about when he'd come home from work."

"I'm sure I'll hear them all eventually."

By then, Mike had clearly established his dominion over the barbecue grill, and Ray was handing out burgers and franks to everyone. He and I sat down together to eat at a pair of Adirondack chairs set back from the kids and moms at the picnic table. Roby knew his people—he settled below Addie and Owen, waiting for slipped or dropped bits of food.

We were getting ready to leave when the ten o'clock news came on, and we shunted the kids to bed with Cathy and Julie while Mike, Ray and I sat in the living room in front of the TV.

"The search continues for a missing fourteen-year-old boy with dangerous behavioral problems," the anchor intoned. "Here's Ralph Kim with the latest update."

He shifted to Ralph, standing in front of the Alapai Headquarters where I worked. Spotlights illuminated him against the dark bulk of the building. Palm trees whipped sharply overhead as he reminded viewers of Charles's disappearance and the discovery of his mother's body. "If you encounter Charles Fontenot, either in a park or on a city street, do not engage him. He should be considered a dangerous individual."

"He's a scared fourteen-year-old boy!" I said.

"Who may have killed his mother," Ray added. "I don't think it's a bad thing to tell people to stay away from him and call the cops instead."

"Did you hear Ralph Kim say that? No. All he said is the poor kid is dangerous."

"Boys, boys," Mike said. "Let's not start this new working relationship the wrong way."

"Thank you, home husband," Ray said.

"You're welcome, work husband."

I just growled.

Ralph continued, "Police sources have indicated that there are currently over one hundred people missing in our state and national parks. And that it's possible many of them have come to a dangerous end."

"Oh, no, he didn't go there," Mike said.

"Authorities caution calm, of course," Ralph said. "But KVOL wants our viewers to know what's going on in the world around us. Until this case is resolved, we urge you to be cautious in hiking or climbing in any of our large parks."

"I'd like to hit him in the head with a rock," I said. "But remind me not to tell my brother that or it'll end up on the news somehow."

Ray turned to me. "Did you tell Lui about the missing people in the parks?"

"I was trying to deflect attention from people thinking Charles is a murderer. He could just be lost, like those other hundred people."

Mike and Ray just looked at me. "I know, I should know by now how my brother and his monkeys will twist anything around. My bad."

Ray turned to Mike. "You see what I have to put up with?"

Mike said, "Welcome back to my world."

Chapter 11
Arrival

Friday morning Ray walked down the hill from Sandra and Cathy's to ride in with me, since it was going to take them a few days to sort out their car situation. It was awesome to have him back at the desk across from mine. Almost as if he'd never left.

We went to the eight o'clock briefing together. "Now that we have isolated the area where Charles is missing, search and rescue teams have come in to take over the hunt for Charles. So we are going back to normal operations."

There was a smattering of applause. "A few notes before I let you go," Queen continued. "Welcome back Detective Ray Donne, who has rejoined HPD after a stint on the mainland."

Lots of calls and waves, to which Ray responded.

"And finally, now that we can relax a bit, the going-away party for Detective Steve Hart is definitely a go, this evening at 6 PM at Samoa House in Waikiki. Be prepared for an evening of music, dance and general revelry."

The meeting broke up, but Sampson indicated that he wanted me and Ray in his office. "Despite the presence of search and rescue,' our involvement in this case is not over. I want you two to focus on it.

It's possible that once we find Charles, this may move into homicide territory, and I want us to be prepared."

"Do you think we'll find Charles Fontenot alive?" Ray asked.

"My gut feeling is yes," Sampson said. "I can easily see Karen Fontenot falling and her son unable to deal, and running away. From what I understand he has some survival skills. It's a strong possibility that he's simply hiding right now."

"But equally strong that he pushed his mother down that slope?" I asked.

"That's what I want you gentlemen to work on." He looked down at the paperwork on his desk, the sign that we were dismissed, and we walked back to our desks.

"I've got a meeting with HR this morning," Ray said. "But I should be back at my desk by noon."

He left, and a few minutes later Doc Takayama's office called with the results of the medical-legal autopsy on Karen Fontenot. "You'll probably want to come see this one in person," his receptionist told me, and I agreed I could be there in half an hour. I wished that Ray could go with me, but we often split up responsibilities like this.

I drove over to Iwilei Road and was directed back to Doc's office.

"Hello, Kimo," he said. "You're here about Karen Fontenot, aren't you?"

"I am indeed. What do you have for me?"

"There were a number of scrapes and bruises on the body, as well as torn clothing, which suggests a tumble down the ravine where she was found, including a severe bruise to the head."

He shifted his screen so I could see and pointed to a photograph of the side of Karen Fontenot's head. Someone had carefully combed away the hair so a large black and blue bruise was visible. "This one worries me," he said. "There were shreds of ironwood in the surrounding hair, which suggests one of two things."

I had learned not to rush Doc when he was in lecture mode.

"One, in the course of rolling down the hill, she banged her head on a piece of wood hard enough to embed fragments. That's not unreasonable, because the crime scene techs climbed that hill and found traces of blood on various pieces of wood."

"Better them than me," I said, imagining crawling up that ravine in the heat and humidity, moving by inches and scanning for blood.

"The other possibility is that someone hit her on the head with a piece of ironwood, knocking her down into the ravine."

I thought about that for a moment as Doc remained silent. I had climbed those mountains myself, sliding down slopes and climbing back up. "I'm thinking out loud here," I said. "If I were at the top of the ravine and I lost my footing, I'd fall down on my butt and go sliding, right?"

"You've been there, so I'll agree."

"But if someone hit me on the back of the head, I might fall forward, and go down on my front."

"Equally a possibility. However, I'd say that the injuries on the victim are more consistent with a downward trajectory on her back."

I nodded. "But it's also possible, isn't it, that someone hit her, she flailed about for a minute, and lost her balance, and went down on her butt, right?"

"That is a valid speculation. But I am very tempted to call this death by misadventure, because the evidence supports that as much as it supports murder or manslaughter."

I sat back in my chair, considering. "If you call it death by misadventure, then we release the body and the family goes home. No need to interview any of them as suspects." I steepled my fingers and twirled my thumbs, as I'd seen my father do so many times when he was thinking.

"The mayor and the tourist board won't be very happy, because if she fell from a marked trail, that will imply safety concerns in our parks and along our climbing trails."

Doc watched me as I spoke.

"But if you presented a tentative verdict of manslaughter, which you said is equally supported by the evidence, then I'd have some time to interview witnesses, search for motives and verify alibis. An extra couple of days would give us a chance to find Charles Fontenot and interview him."

Doc smiled. "And if I do eventually record this as death by misadventure, then you'll be able to prove to the mayor that you did everything you could to investigate."

"Doc, you should be in politics."

Chapter 12
Family History

When Ray came back from HR, I showed him the autopsy results. "I got a very strange vibe when I went to meet the family and told them about Karen's death," I said. "I think we need to know more about their history in order to understand what's going on today. How about we start with this historical home where they live."

I typed Terre Riche Plantation into the search engine and got several pages of results. "Let's alternate. I'll take the odd results, starting with number one. You take the even."

"I always knew you were a little odd."

I pretended to smack my hand across his face and we both laughed. It was good to have him back.

The first result I found explained how the plantation had been founded in 1792 by French settlers Henri and Louise Fontenot. It had been built in a French creole style, with tall columns across the front which stretched for two floors, providing a shady first-floor patio and balconies that spanned the entire front of the house.

The Fontenots planted acres of sugar cane and used slaves to harvest it, and quickly became one of the wealthiest families in the Louisiana Territory. The house had survived the Great Algiers Fire of 1895 because of a narrow canal, since paved over, which ran beside the house and provided water to fight the fire.

But as the centuries wore on, the Fontenot family fell on hard times, and began selling off outbuildings and parcels. Today the plantation was one of the last of its kind still in the hands of the same family.

The last Fontenot before slavery was abolished, Gabriel, was particularly randy, and there were many mixed-race Fontenot descendants, including a group that had traced their ancestry there. The family tree they had created was open to the public.

Off to one side were the white descendants, with a line to Belle's husband Henri, his marriage to her, and their children and grandchildren. Off to the other side were lines from two "enslaved women," Ruth and Judith.

Ruth had two daughters: Eve (1848) and Miriam (1850). who were both listed as "mulatto." Ruth apparently died in childbirth in 1852. In 1855, both her girls were sold at a slave auction at the Banks Arcade in New Orleans. Nothing further was indicated about them.

I stopped there for a moment to consider. Those poor little girls had been born into slavery and lost their mother at an early age. They had been raised in their father's home, probably by another slave woman, and then sold off like cattle or horses. I could only hope that once they landed at another house, they had been treated well and lived until manumission, when they'd been free to assume new lives.

It looked like after Ruth's passing, Gabriel had moved on to Judith. She bore him two sons, Solomon (1855) and Reuben (1857). Both were identified in the records as "creole." I had to stop and look up the difference between creole and mulatto.

The common distinction was that mulatto meant having one white parent and one black parent. Creole seemed a less pejorative term, and meant that you were from French or Spanish background. Sometimes white men freed their mixed-race children, and they were called creoles of color.

Solomon and Reuben were freed in 1864, when slavery was abolished under the Louisiana state constitution. The 1870 census, however, indicated that both of them remained at Terre Riche.

Solomon died in 1874, according to the family tree, but Reuben went on to marry a woman named Mary Smith, who was listed as a quadroon, or one-quarter black.

They had four children. I was getting too emotional, thinking of the lives these people had lived, and I skimmed down, until I came to the last of Solomon's descendants, a boy named Charles who was born in 2000. His father was Omari Fontenot, a single man who had no other children.

I jumped back to the white side of the family. There was no father listed for Karen's son Charles, also born in 2000.

Were there two boys named Charles Fontenot, both born in the same year? Or had Karen sought out her distant cousin to father her child?

"Ray. This is weird."

Ray looked over, and I handed him my iPad. "Look at the last line on both trees."

"Interesting." Without saying more, he turned back to his laptop and typed. "Omari Fontenot lives in Oakland, California, and drives an Uber cab. According to the photo accompanying his license, he's a light-skinned gentleman, but dark enough that he's clearly Black."

Without looking up at me, he grabbed his phone. "I wonder if the state of Louisiana can confirm anything." He called the Louisiana Department of Health, identified himself as a law enforcement officer, and asked how he could get a birth certificate for Charles Fontenot.

I turned back to the family tree and considered what Karen Fontenot had done. If I was correct, she had deliberately sought out a cousin from the slave side of the family to father her son. Did he know who she was, and what she was planning?

I heard Ray say, "Yes, you can call the main number there on your screen. Ask for me—let me spell my name for you." Then I was surprised to hear him spell mine instead.

"Yes, Kimo's a pretty common name here in the islands. When the missionaries came here, they wanted to translate the Bible but there are only twelve consonants in the Hawaiian language. So they just used the next available letter, and the J in James became a K."

I started to laugh. Ray had certainly remembered a lot from his years in Honolulu. "And every word in Hawaiian has to end in a vowel, did you know that? So James became Kimo."

He hung up the phone and looked at me. "I couldn't give my name because I'm sure I'm not in the directory yet. I've only been working here for two hours."

"I'm not laughing at that. The tourist board might want to hire you as an ambassador, if Sampson can't get your hire through."

He held up his first three fingers and said, "Read between the lines."

I laughed some more and he said proudly, "I learned that from Vinnie."

Eventually a facsimile of Charles Fontenot's original certificate was emailed to my address, and Ray scooted his chair over to look at it with me.

There was a space for father's last name, in which someone had written "Fontenot."

The space for father's first name and second name were empty, however. Skipping down, there was a spot for father's city and state of birth, which was blank, though the father's age at the time of the baby's birth was listed as thirty-one. Karen was thirty-four, and all her information had been provided.

"Any ideas?" I asked Ray.

"Let me check one more thing," he said. "Just a hunch."

His credentials weren't valid yet, so he used mine to log into the database of arrivals and departures at Honolulu International Airport. "OK, this is new," he said. "Omari Fontenot arrived from San Francisco the night before Karen and Charles disappeared."

Chapter 13
Baby Daddy

"This can't be a coincidence," I said. "Charles's long-lost father appears, and the next day his mother is killed and he disappears."

We both turned to our phones and started making calls. It took us a couple of hours, but we discovered that no one using Omari Fontenot's name or credentials had rented a car or checked into a hotel on the island.

"Then where did he go?" Ray asked.

I called the Medical Examiner's Office and spoke to Alice Kanamura. "Aloha, Alice. Howzit?"

"Slow," she said. "Biggest case we've had lately is that missing mother."

"About her. Did they find her cell phone?"

"Yes, but it's banged up. Looks like it was in her pocket when she fell and it got crunched."

"Can you courier it over to us anyway?" I asked. "I need to check her call logs."

She agreed. I turned back to my computer and logged into Facebook. A quick search brought me to Omari Fontenot's page. "Look at this," I said. "He loves to hike and camp outdoors. Checked in at a couple of national parks, liked a bunch of camping gear sites."

"When we came in at the airport the other night, I saw a line of city buses," Ray said. "Any of them head to a place he could be camping?"

We hunted through schedules but the best we could come up with was Sand Island State Recreation area, and that only allowed overnight camping on weekends.

"Maybe we're looking at this the wrong way," I said. "Didn't you say he was an Uber driver?"

"Yup. You know anyone who works at the Uber office in Honolulu?"

"A guy I went to Punahou with runs the Uber Greenlight Hub downtown. Let me give him a call."

Eric San Roman and I had both been part of the surf club, so when I finally got him on the phone we talked about surfing for a couple of minutes. Then I said, "Listen, brah, I'm hoping you can help me track someone who might have grabbed an Uber from the airport on Sunday night."

"Let me check the records. What's the guy's name?"

"Omari Fontenot." I spelled it for him, and heard his fingers on the keyboard. "Yeah, he got a ride from the airport shortly before midnight, out to the Malaekahana Beach Campground in Kahuku."

"Awesome, brah. Thanks for your help." Then I remembered something. "Those campgrounds are closed on Wednesday and Thursday nights. Did anyone pick him up there on Wednesday?"

More typing. "Yeah, Wednesday afternoon he went from Kahuku to Manoa. An address on Seaview Avenue."

He gave it to me, and I typed it into a map program. "Bingo," I said. "It's a hostel. Thanks, brah."

I called the hostel, and discovered that Omari Fontenot had checked in on Wednesday, and was still registered.

"Let's go visit the baby daddy," I said, pushing my chair back. It was a windy day, palm fronds tossing, trash skittering along the side of the road.

As we walked out to my SUV, Ray said, "We've been having some problems with Vinnie."

"What kind of problems?"

"Not so much something wrong with him, but what to do with him," he said. "I know you probably have some stereotypical idea of an Italian grandmother, right? Big boobs, little mustache, always welcoming and cooking something."

"Maybe I did, once, but then I heard about Dakota's grandmother. Tough as nails, smokes like a chimney, starts drinking at five o'clock and doesn't stop until bedtime."

"Neither of Vinnie's grandmothers are that bad. My mom retired at sixty-two, last year, and I figured Vinnie could spend some time there after school. But she and her sister started going to the casinos. They'd get on these big buses of senior citizens, get a voucher for the lunch buffet, and ten dollars in play money to start gambling with."

He shook his head. "According to my mom, she usually breaks even, and she says playing blackjack keeps her brain sharp. Julie's mom still works. What started to happen was Vinnie was done with school at 3:00, and we didn't want him home alone at his age."

"Don't they have clubs and activities after school?"

"Not really until middle school, which started this fall. Julie's job was in Center City Philadelphia, and she had to work at least until five, and then catch a commuter train. Not home until six o'clock at the earliest. And I was on the afternoon shift, three-thirty to midnight."

"You couldn't switch?"

"Nah, I was lucky to get that. The way they run things in the township where I was, there are two districts. One detective per district per shift, with a detective sergeant to help run things. My sergeant thought he was going to get the promotion, so he was pissed as all hell when I showed up. He wouldn't walk me through any procedures, any paperwork. We got into this long-time pissing match.

Whenever something went wrong, I blamed him because he didn't give me the heads up. And he blamed me because I was the boss."

"Ouch."

"I had no flex time to devote to Vinnie either. Julie found this "enrichment" program after school, and she signed him up for that. Turns out it was more like remedial work for slow kids, and he was bored out of his mind and started acting up. Then every so often Julie would be late to pick him up, and the woman who ran it gave her holy hell."

His body sagged. "You have no idea how stressful it was. Both of us in new jobs, neither of us happy. And Vinnie starting to melt down."

"What did you do?"

"The woman finally gave Julie an ultimatum. Take Vinnie out or never be late again. So we pulled him out. He had this friend with a stay-at-home mom, and we made a deal with her that Vinnie could go home with his friend."

"That's good."

"Yeah, except the friend had an older brother, and after a week there Vinnie came to me and said, 'Dad, you always told me to tell you if someone was acting weird.'"

"Oh, no."

Ray sighed. "The older brother wanted to play games in their undies, and Vinnie said no."

"Good for him."

"Yeah, but it left us with not only the problem of what to do with him, but what to tell the friend's mom."

"You had to tell her the truth."

"I know. And we did, and she flipped out, accused Vinnie of being the instigator. Ruined Vinnie's only friendship. We started cobbling together whatever we could, neighbors, cousins, paying babysitters. But it wasn't sustainable. Then Julie's mentor called her about this job, and it seemed like the answer to our prayers."

We drove in silence for a couple of minutes. "I love that kid so much. I will do whatever it takes to make him happy."

"That's a tough call," I said. "I've wrestled with that same concept for years. I think that we can make them feel trusted, loved and safe. Because Vinnie was able to come to you with that problem, you can feel good about those. You can make sure he always has a roof over his head and food in his stomach. You can be there to help him achieve his potential in sports, academics, whatever he wants."

I turned to look at him. "But you can't make him happy."

He cocked his head. "Why not?"

"Because happiness has to come from inside, brah. You know that. You give him all the rest, and you hope that it's what he needs." I shook my head. "Charles Fontenot, there's something wrong with his brain, and no amount of parental care can cure that."

"Like I told Sampson, I have a lot of experience with that kind of kid. I hated my job so much that I took every chance I could for extra training. If it got me out of the squad room, I was happy." He looked down at his lap. "Every time I took one I'd come home and examine Vinnie. If he fought us about going to bed, was that a sign of something more?"

"That must have been tough."

"Julie and I argued about it, too. She told me I was helicoptering, even though I hardly spent any time with him. That my constant fear made her feel like she wasn't doing a good enough job as a mom to meet my standards."

"Oh, boy."

He looked up. "This move is going to be good for all of us. I need a positive work environment, and Julie needs more flexibility in her schedule, which teaching will give her. She'll be her own boss regarding the research, so she can work at home if she wants outside of her regular office hours at UH. We won't have a huge issue over taking Vinnie to a doctor's appointment or watching him in a school play or a ball game."

"It's been easier with four of us," I admitted. "Mike and I had to step up with Sandra in DC so much, but still, there's always one of us who can do whatever needs doing. And I want you to count on us, too. When I take the keikis swimming or surfing, it's no problem to take Vinnie, too. And Owen's going out for Little League this spring —Vinnie can join the same team so there's always someone from his ohana there to cheer him on, even if you and Julie can't make it."

There was such a sense of gratitude in his face that it made my heart leap. "This is why we wanted to be back here," he said. "For all of you, of course. But for this sense of ohana, that Vinnie will grow up part of a larger family that will always have his back. I wish Julie and I felt that way about our blood family."

The hostel was located on a side street off the University of Hawai'i campus. Students hurried to classes, their heads down against the trade winds, and one unfortunate guy chased pages that had fallen out of his backpack. The hostel looked like a big old house that had been converted, with a broad front porch and white columns. The hipped roofs looked like they had weathered many hurricanes.

I showed my badge to a clerk in the lobby and asked for Omari Fontenot.

"He's right outside," the clerk said, and pointed through a window to a back patio. A light-skinned Black man sat at the table texting.

"Mr. Fontenot?" I asked, as we walked outside. I introduced myself and Ray, and showed him my badge. "We'd like to talk to you about your son, Charles."

"Thank God," he said. "He hasn't been returning my calls or texts. I've been so worried."

Ray and I sat down across the table from him. "I guess you haven't seen the local news?" I asked.

He shook his head. "Is there something wrong?"

"He's missing," I said. "He and his mother went hiking on Monday." I paused. "Karen's body was found on Wednesday, but there has been no sign of Charles."

His eyes widened and his mouth dropped open. "That's terrible."

"Can you tell us how you came to be here?" Ray asked.

Omari nodded. "Sure. So this all started about two years ago. My cousin created a family tree online for the Black descendants of the Fontenot line. She added me, and then put in Charles's name too—though without my knowledge or permission."

He took a deep breath. "I guess I need to step back even further. About fifteen years ago, a woman contacted me by phone. She said her name was Karen Fontenot, that she was from New Orleans, and she'd been doing some genealogy work and discovered me and my branch of the family. She was coming to San Francisco on a business trip and asked if we could meet."

He looked down at the table. But both Ray and I knew not to rush him. "We met for cocktails, which segued into dinner, which then... well, we went back to her hotel room." He looked up. "We were only very distant cousins, but there was a spark between us. Some kind of shared family heritage. I liked her, though she was, I guess you'd say brittle. Then I went home and she went to her meetings, and the next day she flew back to Louisiana."

"I know this is awkward question," Ray asked. "But you'll understand why I ask. Did you use any protection when you had sex with her?"

Omari shook his head. "She said she was on the pill, and I believed her. Then about a year later she called me late one night and told me that she'd had a child, a son. He was named Charles after one of her grandfathers. She was drunk, and I couldn't get much more information out of her except that she was sure the boy was my son."

"What did you do after that?" I asked.

"I called her back a couple of days after that, but she didn't answer. I tried several more times and each time I couldn't reach her and I left messages. Eventually I realized that she didn't want anything to do with me. Because I'd never seen the boy, or even a picture, it was easy to push him out of my mind."

A plane flew overhead, on its way to land at HNL. "I tried, you know. I really did," Omari said, when it had passed. "But what else could I do? Fly to New Orleans and demand to see him? I was barely getting by and I didn't have that kind of money, and from what I understood she was very wealthy, so I knew she'd take care of him."

"And then?" Ray asked.

"About a year ago, I got an email from Charles. He'd tracked me down through that genealogy website and wanted to know if I was his father. He wasn't very polite about it, but eventually I learned that's the way he was. I wrote back and explained the circumstances, and we started to correspond occasionally. Most of the time he wanted to complain about his mother and his relatives, how much he hated studying and so on. I tried to be encouraging, especially once he shared his diagnosis with me."

"How did you know he and his family would be in Hawai'i?" I asked.

"Charles told me. He asked me to meet him here. He wanted me to meet his mother again, and the rest of his family. He knew that I liked to hike and camp, and he hoped we could spend some time together."

Ray nodded. "When was the last time you heard from him?"

"I got a text from him the morning after I landed. That was Monday. He and his mother were going hiking that morning. He said he'd call me when they got back, and we'd set up a meeting."

"You didn't go out to meet Karen and Charles where they were hiking?" I asked.

He shook his head. "He didn't say where they were going. I tried calling him that afternoon, and then I've been calling and texting every day since, without any answer. I was camping out in a park, to save money, but Wednesday morning they said I had to leave, so I came here. You can check with the clerk. I haven't left except to get some food locally. I don't have a car and I don't know how the buses work here."

He looked at us. "Are you telling me that Charles has been missing since he last texted me? Are you looking for him?"

"We are," I said. "I'm the one who found Karen's body on

Wednesday, and since then we've had search and rescue teams combing that park looking for Charles. But we understand that because of his condition he may be hiding from the searchers."

A look of anguish crossed his face. "I wish I had known. I could help with the searching."

"You aren't planning to leave Honolulu yet, are you?" I asked.

He shook his head. "I have a return ticket in a week. After that I need to get back to work."

I took his cell phone number and promised we'd call him when we found Charles. "In the meantime, if you hear from him, please let us know."

We walked back to where I'd parked. "Do you believe him?" Ray asked.

"It all sounds very logical," I said. "And if he was at the Malaekahana Beach Campground in Kahuku on Monday, when Karen and Charles went hiking, there isn't an easy way for him to get to St. Louis Heights except via Uber, and we know he didn't call one until Wednesday morning when he had to leave the campground."

"Or Karen could have picked him up on her way," he said.

"That's true. But that implies that he was with them on the trail and then something happened and Karen went down. You're a father. Even if you and Vinnie were estranged, would you have left him alone under those circumstances?"

Ray shook his head. "At the very least I would have taken him out of the park. But you're letting your personal feelings as a father get in the way. Let's say that Omari isn't as nice as he appears."

He leaned back against the window and let the air conditioning blast his face. "Without confirmation from Charles why Omari is here in the first place, we can't completely understand his motives. Suppose, for example, that Charles told him about this vacation but didn't specifically invite him. Omari shows up, unexpected. Maybe he spoke to Karen before she went out hiking with Charles on Monday."

"What would that conversation have been like?" I asked.

"Maybe he tells Karen he's planning to claim Charles as his son. Sue for joint custody."

"We have been told Karen was very protective of Charles," I admitted. "That would freak her out."

"Looking up the Fontenots in New Orleans, seeing that mansion they live in, Omari assumes they've got money. Maybe he doesn't want custody, just a payout to keep his mouth shut. Maybe Belle doesn't want to advertise the fact that her grandson has a Black father—and one descended from the family slaves at that."

"Let's walk this through," I said. "Omari says that he texted Charles the morning he and his mother went missing. What if Karen drove out to the campground and picked Omari up, and they all went hiking together."

"And somewhere along the trail, maybe when Charles has wandered off, Omari tells Karen what he wants."

I nodded. "They argue, she falls or he pushes her. He runs away. Sure, most people on O'ahu get around by car, but you can always get somewhere if you really have to. Harry and I used to hitchhike to the North Shore carrying surfboards. Maybe Omari met somebody on the plane, swapped phone numbers, and called that stranger for a ride. Went back to the campground."

"Why not leave Honolulu immediately?" Ray asked.

"Two possible reasons. One, with Karen dead, he's the boy's legal father, which strengthens his case for custody or money. And two, he's admitted he doesn't have that much money himself, so maybe he couldn't afford changing a plane ticket at the last minute. Instead he hides out at the hostel."

Ray turned to face me. "I see your point. But no matter what happened to Karen, whether she fell or slipped or was pushed, I don't think Omari would have left Charles behind."

"Even if he killed Karen?"

"Unless Charles actually witnessed Omari push Karen down the slope, Omari could have argued it was an accident."

I wasn't sure about that. "As a Black man accused of killing a white woman?"

"I admit, if I were Omari and I was in that situation I'd be very worried," Ray said. "He didn't really know Charles or know what he'd say under interrogation. But this is all supposition—I feel very strongly that Omari wasn't there, because he would never have left Charles in the park alone."

"My experience of fatherhood agrees with you. But my experience as a cop says don't rule anyone out until you have a suspect and a confession."

Chapter 14
Samoa House

We drove back to headquarters just in time for an impromptu meeting called by Queen. "Thank you all for your dedicated work over the last couple of days. Charles Fontenot was found in Wa'ahila Ridge State Recreation Area about an hour ago by the search and rescue team. He is being checked over at the Queen's Medical Center. Early indications are that he's dehydrated and traumatized, but otherwise healthy."

I raised my hand. "When will we be able to speak to him about what happened?"

"Right now, he's non-verbal, which the doctors say is normal given his condition and the experience he's been through. They will notify us as soon as he's able to talk."

We reported to Sampson what we'd found, and he agreed that it was too early to attempt a case against Omari Fontenot. "I'm stretching my budget as far as I can hiring Detective Donne," he said. "So that means we let the weekend pass before you go back to the Fontenot investigation. Give the boy a chance to recover and reconnect with his family. Kick things off again on Monday morning."

Before we left I checked with Mary Luo, who was coordinating the going-away party for Steve Hart. She confirmed that it was fine if

I brought a plus-one. I had already paid a week before, so I handed her the twenty-five bucks for Ray.

Mike would have been welcome at the party—he knew a lot of the people that I worked with, either through me or through his work at the fire department—but he said he'd rather stay home.

"When does Julie start work?" I asked, as we drove toward Waikiki.

"Like about an hour after she accepted the job," he said. "She has to teach what they call a two-two load, which means two classes in the fall and two in the spring. Walsh, the guy she's replacing, had already been scheduled for two in the fall, and they were cancelled, so when they were rescheduled for the spring they filled up quickly. He passed on his reading lists and his syllabi, so Julie has been scrambling to get up to speed."

"And doesn't she have research projects too?"

"Walsh had some good grad students who've been keeping up with the data collection. But Julie's going to have a massive amount to do to catch up with all that, too."

He looked over at me. "I haven't seen her so happy, though, for years. And that makes all this upset worth it."

A couple of years before, Mike had been offered a job as assistant fire chief, a step up from his position as a fire investigator. He had been reluctant to take it, because there was something about fire that intrigued him, that called to him from somewhere deep inside.

He wasn't a pyromaniac or anything like that—he didn't want to start fires that hurt anyone or destroyed anything. But he loved the science of it, understanding how it started, how it grew, how it moved through time and space. He worried that moving into administration would take him a big step farther away from the thing that had attracted him to the job.

I tried to explain that to Ray, but couldn't find the right words, which frustrated me. "He waffled over the decision for days. Went on hikes by himself. Even barked at the dog."

"Obviously he made the decision, though."

"He did. I think one reason he wouldn't talk about it with me was because part of him said it was the adult, safe thing to do. That he was doing it for me, and the kids, to pull himself out of danger."

"It is what you do when you love someone."

"But you and I haven't done that." I turned to him as the familiar landscape of the H2 highway sped past us. Palm trees and industrial buildings, a spray of pink bougainvillea and a billboard for KHON radio. "We're both big boys playing cops and robbers."

"I wouldn't phrase it quite like that," Ray said. "I prefer to think of myself as a shield between bad actors and good people."

I laughed. "Makes you sound like a movie critic."

"Seriously. What pushed him over the edge?"

"I don't know. But within a couple of weeks, he was loving the job. Turns out the one thing he likes more than investigating fires is teaching people about fire. Sure, he does his share of paperwork, but his gig is being in charge of training, and the fire investigators work under him. He gets to do all the geeky stuff he loves without the risk."

"And he's happy?"

"Oh, yeah. And I am, too. Not worrying about his safety every time a call comes in."

"Julie has this fantasy that I'll get a job with a private security agency someday," he said. "A supervisor, running a team of guards at some luxury enclave."

I turned to look at him. "You'd hate that."

He nodded. "But I'd do it if it means making Julie happy."

"Is she happy you've come back to HPD?"

"Right now she's so grateful we could come back here so she can remake her life, and Vinnie's, that she'll agree to almost anything."

I got off the H2 at the Kapahulu Avenue entrance, so we could bypass much of the traffic into Waikiki, and managed to get a parking spot close to Samoa House, which was a few blocks away on Kuhio Avenue.

It was a big tourist trap in Polynesian style, lots of grass roofs and tiki statues. But it was one of the few places where you could get a large private room at a significant law enforcement discount. And I was looking forward to seeing a big haole guy like Steve Hart embarrassed by tiers of leis, being drawn on stage by a couple of scantily dressed wahines and forced to dance.

Mary Luo was outside the door taking names. She checked us off and said, "*Welina hou.*" Then she had to turn to the next guy in line.

Ray looked at me. "My Hawaiian's gotten kind of rusty."

"Welcome back," I said. "I'm sure you're going to hear that a lot tonight."

That was the case. We got a couple of beers and began to work the room. Ray and Julie had only been gone for a couple of years, but the two years before that Ray and I had been assigned to the Joint Terrorism Task Force, working hand-in-hand with the FBI and other agencies. There were some folks he'd never met, and others he hadn't seen in years, and we had a good time.

While Ray was engaged in a debate about island versus mainland policing, Queen Jones cornered me. I had known her for a couple of years by then, as a cheerful organizer, a stalwart when there were any big events or visiting celebrities who needed police escorts, and an out lesbian who volunteered with at-risk kids.

"Do you have a minute? I want to talk with you about coal."

I cocked my head. As far as I knew, we used oil, natural gas, and wind and wave energy to generate power in Hawaii. Not coal.

"Q-O-L-E," she clarified. "Queer Oahu Law Enforcement. A new employee resource group I'm starting in the department."

For a moment my heart raced, and I remembered the moment, fourteen years before, when I had walked into a conference room in the Alapai Headquarters and met with my then-boss and a union representative and acknowledged that I was gay. It was one of the first times I'd spoken that word out loud, and I still recalled how much import it had carried.

At the time I was the only out detective at HPD, but times had changed a lot since then. More gay, bi, and pan employees had come out, and the department's hiring policies had encouraged more to join us. I was uncomfortable with the spotlight, though I knew I had an important role to play, and I was glad when I'd been able to slide back into my ordinary life.

There had still been slurs cast behind my back, of course. There were other cops, mostly older ones, who refused to work with me. Every so often an online squib about a case I'd been involved with reminded readers that I was a homosexual.

"We need representation in the upper ranks," she said, as chatter and music ebbed and flowed around us.

"I'm not management, I'm a detective."

"You're a detective sergeant," she said. "I've already recruited Captain Quinn, and I don't want him to be the only member above patrol level."

She pulled a typed list from her pocket and handed it to me. Nicholas Quinn, head of the Traffic Enforcement Division for District 2. He was the highest-ranking gay officer I knew on the force. Her name was below his, and then another ten names, almost half male and half female. I knew two of them.

Jeremy Hoult was a patrol officer in District 1, where I was based. And Kitty Cardozo had just passed her sergeant's exam but she was waiting for a detective spot to open up. Until then she was a shift supervisor in district three, encompassing the neighborhood where Mike and I lived.

She was also Lieutenant Sampson's stepdaughter. "Have you thought about opening membership up to friends and family, like PLFAG?" I asked Queen. "You could get some higher-ranking folks to join that way."

"We're going to invite them to events, but for now we want to limit membership to openly serving members. We're reaching out to the coroner's office, the fire department, and EMS as well."

I knew what was coming next.

"I'm hoping you'll ask your partner to join us, too. Isn't he the ranking gay member at HFD?"

"He is. But I don't know that his bosses will want him to participate."

She smiled. "You'd be surprised at what the public relations departments want from all of us these days."

I had been much more visible when I was younger, marching in pride parades and serving as the department's representative on various projects. I'd mentored an LGBT youth group in Waikiki for a couple of years, until I moved into Mike's house in Aiea Heights and we focused on building our relationship, and then our family.

"How much of a time commitment are you asking for?"

"An organizational meeting first. Then we're thinking about occasional social activities, and community outreach on an as-needed basis."

"I'll do it," I said. "And I'll ask Mike tonight."

Sampson arrived, somebody got him a beer and someone else adjusted the microphone to handle his height, and then the room got quiet.

"I've been asked to come up and say a few words about Steve Hart," he said. "Tall. Californian. Likes to surf." He took a swig of his beer. "That few enough for you?"

The crowd laughed. Sampson told a couple of quasi-embarrassing anecdotes about Steve, and then Steve came up and thanked the crowd for coming to say goodbye. "I'm sure there are some of you who wished this party had happened a long time ago."

Perhaps he was looking at me, or maybe just in my general direction. We'd had a few bust-ups in our time, and though he could occasionally be lazy, I thought he was a decent cop and a good investigator.

As he finished, the drumbeats sounded, and we all turned to the front door. A pair of burly Samoans beating drums came in, leading a pair of shapely young women of indeterminate Asian ancestry, who danced their way in.

I was more interested in the Samoans, of course, who had muscular, tattooed chests and impressive thighs only modestly covered by their grass skirts. I had discovered long ago that they usually wore jock straps beneath those skirts, and I was thinking of that when Ray elbowed me.

"Eyes in your head."

I looked at him. "Pot. Black."

We both laughed, and I remembered how easy our working relationship had been. I needed that again, and I knew Ray did, too.

The dancers joined Steve Hart on stage. He had obviously expected this, and to his credit he did a pretty good job of following their steps. The crowd cheered, and I couldn't tell if they were happy he could dance, or sorry he wasn't making a fool of himself.

Ray and I stayed at Samoa House for another hour, and then we decided we'd had enough. I was driving us back to Aiea Heights when my cell phone rang through the Jeep's Bluetooth. "Greg Oshiro," Ray said when he saw the display. "There's a blast from the past."

Greg was an investigative reporter for the *Honolulu Star-Bulletin*, and he'd frequently called both of us to ferret out information about ongoing cases.

I hit the button to accept the call. "Aloha, Greg. How are the girls?" Some years before, he'd donated sperm to a lesbian couple, as Mike and I had done. After one of the moms had been murdered, he'd moved the other mom and the girls into his house.

"Ana's mural business is doing well, and the keikis are enjoying school," he said. "How's your ohana?"

"All good," I said. "What can I do for you this fine evening?"

"I understand you're investigating the death of that tourist up in Wa'ahila Ridge Park. Is her son a suspect?"

"You know as well as I do that information has to come from Media and Public Relations. I can't comment on an ongoing case."

"But you talk to your brother, don't you? Print media is dying, Kimo, and we need a level playing field with television. You're the one who found her body, aren't you? What can you tell me?"

"That climbing mountains is dangerous, especially for visitors to our islands who don't know the landscape or the vegetation."

"Kimo."

"What do you want me to tell you, Greg? You already know that her body was found at the bottom of a steep slope and had to be airlifted out of the park." I'd read that in Greg's morning article.

"Do you suspect the son? Staff at the Albergo d'Italia heard him screaming like a banshee. He wouldn't eat in the hotel restaurant with the rest of the family."

"Greg. You're treading very dangerously on the privacy of teenaged boy. A boy who just lost his mother."

"Who he might have pushed down a very steep hill."

"Good night, Greg." I hit the button to end the call.

"So much for your polish with the fourth estate," Ray said. "I see that hasn't changed."

"He can call the police press contact," I said. "I'm not going to violate a teenager's privacy to satisfy the public's demand for salacious news."

I dropped Ray off and circled back to the house. When I found Mike in the living room, I said, "Sampson doesn't want Ray and me to get back to the Fontenot case until Monday. I would love to enjoy the weekend with the keikis."

"Great idea," Mike said. "What do you want to do?"

"I was thinking incorporating some basic research into the case while having some fun and wearing the kids out. Let me think about where to go. There's one more thing, though."

I told Mike about my conversation with Queen and conveyed her request. I was surprised when he agreed so readily. "We're role models, K-Man," putting down his iPad. "Whether we want to be or not. We owe it to the officers and fire fighters and staff members who need to see people like us above them. We can lobby for change, within our departments and with the general public."

"I'm tired of being a poster boy," I said. "Been there, done that, got the T-shirt and wore it out."

"It's never going to stop, so get over yourself."

I was irritated, so I sat down at my laptop to see if I could make any progress on the case. Though I wasn't drunk, and I'd been fine to drive home from Waikiki, my brain still felt fuzzy. I knew there was a Facebook group for missing persons in Hawaii, and I started there, to see if I could get any ideas.

Sadly, the cases were too vague, or too different, to be much help. An elderly man who had wandered away from an assisted living facility. A soldier missing from Schofield Barracks, who had been located. A brother who had been living homeless in Wahiawa. At first glance, no one who'd been reported missing while on a hike or in a natural area.

I gave up and pushed aside my research and joined Mike in bed, where Roby did his best to interfere in an intimate moment. I finally had to get up, naked and longing, and banish him outside the bedroom, before Mike and I could get back to business.

Saturday morning dawned fresh and clear. I checked by phone on Charles Fontenot. "His cuts and bruises are healing," the nurse I spoke with said. "He can be discharged at any time but his family are still deciding what to do with him. His father was here yesterday afternoon, and he sat with Charles for a couple of hours, but the boy still isn't talking."

I sat back after I heard that. What to do with him? Why, take him back into the family bosom, of course.

Then again, if he had killed his mother, I could see some reluctance on the part of his grandmother and the rest of the family on taking him in.

Chapter 15
Meltdown

I was staring at my cell phone when it startled me by ringing, with my friend Gunter's name on the display.

"You're up awfully early," I said, though it was close to ten. "What's the matter, you didn't get lucky last night?"

"I did, and he stayed for breakfast and the morning paper," Gunter said. "Which is why I'm calling you."

"Was he someone I know?"

"You might. He's a front desk clerk at the Albergo d'Italia in Kahala."

I sat up. "Really?"

"Indeed. We were skimming the paper together and he saw an article about the tourist who died. He checked her family in when they arrived."

"And?"

"He knew the son was trouble. He sat down with one of the potted plants in the lobby and started digging through the dirt and had a tantrum when his uncle pulled him away."

I remembered the information on Charles, and his fascination with trees, leaves and bugs.

"And he told me something else," Gunter said.

"Go on. You know how much I value your insider information."

Though I said it sarcastically, it was true. Gunter had been helpful in a number of my cases in the past. He was a valet, and a keen observer of people. You might say nosy, but he was my friend, so I looked for positives.

"If you're going to take that tone..."

"Gunter. Come on. Please?"

"Well, since you're being nice. The family has run over the credit limit on the card they used to guarantee the room. The old lady doesn't seem to be as rich as she pretends to be. One of the sons had to step in with a card for incidental charges."

That was interesting. When I'd been at the Albergo, I'd been impressed with the quality of the hotel, and the large suite that Belle Fontenot had booked.

"And by the way, you know who I saw last night while I was out and about? That hunky brother-in-law of yours."

I had two brothers, and two sisters-in-law. It took me a moment to realize he was talking about my sister-in-law Tatiana's brother. "Sergei? Is he back in town?"

"You didn't know?"

"I was disconnected from the family grapevine while I was searching the woods." I hesitated, but then dove in. "How did he look? Overweight? Red eyes? Slow on the uptake?"

Sergei was a needle in Tatiana's side. Or more like a hot poker. When he wasn't doped up, incarcerated, or otherwise in trouble, he was bearishly sexy, smart and funny. Too bad that wasn't much of the time.

"On the contrary, he was hot, hot, hot," Gunter said, singing the old Caribbean tune. "He's a fine specimen of a man. If he could get his act together, he's the kind of guy I could take on for more than a one-night stand."

I nearly spluttered, but it made sense. Both Gunter and Sergei were sex on wheels. And it gave me an evil sense of happiness to consider the two of them settled down into the kind of domesticity

Mike and I had. But could they manage no more threesomes, no more drug-enhanced sexuality, a commitment to the same dick and ass and mouth in bed?

Gunter yawned. "Well, I need to get my beauty sleep. I have a Hinge coffee date this afternoon and a Grinder guy booked for later."

"You are a marvel," I said. "I know you're close to my age, Gunter. How do you manage so much sex after forty?"

"Don't say the F word!" he said in mock horror. "I am thirty-something myself. A young-looking thirty-something, at least in my profile pictures. I count on my other attributes to keep a face-to-dick encounter lively."

I laughed and hung up. Gunter was a force of nature.

But hearing about the Fontenot family problems I worried that they might leave the Albergo and head back to New Orleans. I called the hotel, identified myself, and spoke to the manager. "Are the Fontenot family still at the hotel?" I asked.

"They have extended their stay, yes. They are waiting for the Medical Examiner's office to release Ms. Fontenot's body before they depart."

I needed the Fontenots to remain in Honolulu until I had a chance to talk with them, but I couldn't do that until Monday, according to Lieutenant Sampson. I called the ME's office to see when they would be releasing the body, and no one could tell me anything. I had to leave a message for Doc Takayama to call me back.

Mike, Cathy, Julie and I got onto a conference call later and we decided, since the weather was good, to head to Hanauma Bay. We could hike for a while, then take the kids swimming in the shallow water.

We had a great time, though we were not far from Kahala, and the thought that Karen and Charles Fontenot had visited Hanauma Bay soon after they arrived in Honolulu stuck in the back of my head. We did some climbing, and then made our way down to the water.

While the kids were swimming and Cathy and Julie were watching them, I turned to Ray and Mike. "I keep imagining Karen and Charles Fontenot here. Did they have a good time? I know that neither of them could have expected what was going to happen, but it feels almost like this might have been one of their last happy times together."

"You're assuming they were happy," Mike said. "You have any evidence to base that on?"

I shook my head. "When I came here to search for them, all I was looking for was the rental car license plate."

Ray stood up. "You have a badge, even if I haven't gotten mine yet. Why don't we do some investigating?"

"Go," Mike said. "I'm relaxing."

Ray and I walked up to the education center and I showed my ID to the elegant Thai woman in charge, whose name badge read Achara.

"I remember them," she said. "We get all kinds of kids here, you know. Not many teens, unless they're in school groups, because they're too cool for this kind of education. But the boy, he was really into the exhibit on plants and algae. He kept asking all these questions about giant kelp—sophisticated questions for a boy his age."

I looked at Ray. At least the kid had been happy here.

Then Achara continued. "He got frustrated when I couldn't answer some of them. Then his mother tried to get him to move on, but he wouldn't. It was like his feet were glued to the floor."

The edges of her mouth dipped down. "I feel sorry for parents who have kids with special needs. They can be difficult to deal with. This boy started yelling at his mother, even though she was talking very quietly. When she tried to take his arm, he pushed her away, and she nearly fell."

She rubbed her upper arms with her hands. "Then it was like somebody flipped a switch in him. He got all upset, calling her Mommy and apologizing. She took it all in and eventually convinced him to move on."

We thanked her and got her full name and contact information in case we needed to follow up. "That gives us some evidence that

Charles could be violent," I said, as we walked back to where we'd left the family.

"We already knew that, because of the diagnosis of Oppositional Defiant Disorder. Kids in that situation often resort to physical violence like tantrums because they can't stand the disruption in what they want to do."

"Still, it gives us evidence that he's been physical with his mom, and that makes it possible that he could have pushed her off the trail."

"What did the ME say?"

"Tentative ruling of death by misadventure, because all her bruises were consistent with the fall. But I want to make sure that they don't release Karen's body until I get a chance to interview the family. So I put a call in to Doc Takayama."

"I was surprised he wasn't at that party last night. Is he still seeing Lidia Portuondo?"

"Yeah, they got married last year. She made sergeant and got transferred to District 2, and last I knew they were looking at condos near Pearl Harbor. I got the feeling that they don't want kids so they want a condo with a view."

"Everybody makes their own choices."

We were all back together in the parking lot, ready to load into Cathy's SUV and mine, when Addie asked me, "Is it true you saved Mama's life? In a fire?"

It was like one of those movie scenes where everything stops. Cathy and Mike were loading gear into the back of the SUV, while Ray carried a cooler and Julie a couple of lawn chairs. The three kids stood in a ring around me.

"That's true," I said. "Both your mothers and I were at a party, and a bad man caused a fire. I was close to Mama and I pulled her outside with me."

"But you're a p'liceman," Owen said. "Daddy's the fireman."

"Sometimes it takes a few minutes for the truck and the firemen to arrive at the scene of a fire," I said. "I didn't know your Daddy then —that's the night we met—but I didn't have time to wait."

Addie came over and clutched my side, leaning her head against me. "You're a hero."

"Oh, sweetie," I said, and I hoisted her up into my arms. It was like picking up one of those huge bags of dog food we buy for Roby—she was well over fifty pounds. It helped that she wrapped her arms around my neck and snuggled against me.

"What if you hadn't been there?" Owen demanded. "Would we all be dead?"

I looked at Mike.

"Then I would have rescued Mama," he said.

"The universe is a complicated place," Ray said. "Everything that happens has a reason, and an effect on everything afterward. Your Papa K saved your Mama, even though neither of them had even thought of you guys yet. Lots of other things happened in between."

"Did you fall in love with Mama then?" Addie asked.

I shook my head. "Mama and Mommy were already in love." I smiled and reached a hand out to Mike. "But I was all by myself, until I saw a handsome fireman who drove a truck with flames painted on the side." Mike still had that same truck, though it had a lot more miles on it. As did we all.

"Daddy!" Owen crowed as Mike took my hand.

"Yup. I fell in love with Daddy and introduced him to Mama and Mommy." Suddenly the theme to the *Brady Bunch* came into my head. "And we knew that we wanted to make a family together. You and Addie made that dream come true for all of us."

I turned and lifted Addie into the SUV, and Owen clambered in beside her, and everyone else got into the vehicles wherever there was a place for them, and we rode back home together.

We unloaded everyone at Sandra and Cathy's and Mike and I drove home. "Where do you think that came from?" he asked. "About the fire?"

"Who knows? I mean, we've told them stuff before, about how we were all friends and wanted to make a family together. I don't know if we ever mentioned the fire."

"It made me sound a little late to the party," Mike admitted. "Usually fire rescue is my territory."

"Well, you were late that night," I said. "You weren't a firefighter then, you were an investigator. Nobody expected you to be first on the scene and rescue damsels in distress."

"Addie and Owen did."

"Addie and Owen love you so much already they couldn't love you more if you took off your reading glasses one day and announced you're Superman."

I leaned over and kissed his cheek. "And I couldn't either."

Chapter 16
Skewered

Sunday morning, I got a text from Doc Takayama that he and Lidia had taken a couple of days off for a quick trip to Maui, and that he'd be back in the office on Monday. Not to worry; no one was going to release Karen Fontenot's body without his signoff.

Right after that, a second text came in. An invitation to an impromptu luau at Haoa's and Tatiana's that afternoon. Was it to welcome Sergei back to Honolulu? If it was, for once I had a piece of news before the rest of the coconut telegraph got it.

I relayed the message to the rest of the ohana, while Mike went next door to talk to his parents. When I met him, he was single and closeted, and I thought it was either stupid or self-sabotaging to have bought the other half of the duplex where he had grown up. You certainly couldn't hide a one-night stand if your parents could see your driveway from their living room.

But eventually he had come out, and introduced me to them, and his father and I had settled into an uneasy truce, which eventually had become a full-blown father and son relationship, especially after my own father died. Now I was glad to have them nearby.

Once we had affirmative responses from all concerned, I

responded to Liliha's text on behalf of all of us. "We'll be eleven, counting Ray, Julie and Vinnie," I texted. "May have to rent a bus."

She responded with a thumbs up. Being the mother of teens, and then young people, had converted her from calling to texting.

Then I called my mother. "Is someone picking you up for the luau this afternoon?"

"You are the first who has offered."

"That's because I'm the best son," I said, even though I knew that wasn't remotely true. "What are you cooking?"

"Nothing. This party is a big surprise to me. I can't pull a pot of chicken long rice out of a hat like a rabbit, you know."

"Should I make something?"

She laughed. "You can't cook, Kimo."

"Of course I can," I said. "Mike and I alternate making dinner for each other every night."

"That's not cooking, that's preparing," she said. "None of you boys ever showed an interest in learning how to cook."

"We'll see about that," I said. "We'll pick you up at two. Love you."

"I love you too," she said.

I quickly turned to my iPad and Googled quick simple Hawaiian dishes. "Mike," I called. "You can cook beef skewers, can't you?"

"I can grill anything that has a flame involved."

"Great. I'll be right back."

I jumped into my Jeep and zoomed down the hill to the Foodland, where I did a quick shop, buying the ingredients from the online recipe: light brown sugar, soy sauce, pineapple juice, garlic and round steak. I doubled the amount of the recipe. I can do this, I said to myself. Mike and me together.

Then I got home and read the instructions, which included "marinate beef in the refrigerator for 24 hours."

I looked at the clock. I had four hours, not twenty-four.

Oh well, I'd do my best. I was determined to impress my mother. I'd bought a fresh pineapple instead of canned juice, and I carved the shell into boats and decorated them with yellow plumeria blossoms from a tree in our back yard.

"Why are you going to so much trouble?" Mike asked, as I lined up the boats.

"My mother says I can't cook."

"You can't."

I kicked out at him. "Then who feeds you every night?"

"We have take-out, or I barbecue. When was the last time you cooked something?"

"I made you chicken marsala last week."

"With marsala sauce from a jar."

"The mushrooms were fresh! And I sliced the chicken breast myself."

He stared at me and started to laugh. "You are so not a mama's boy," he said.

I laughed with him. "Can I help it if my father was the surfer in the family and that's who I bonded with?"

I was stirring the marinade when my cell phone rang. I picked it up and stuck it under my ear. "Kimo? It's Jim Sampson. Sorry to bother you on a Sunday."

Maybe because he rarely phoned me, and I always thought of him as Lieutenant Sampson, but I had a moment of surprise at the use of his first name.

"No problem," I said.

"Jules Fontenot is getting to be a pain in the mayor's ass," he said. "He keeps calling and demanding the release of his sister's body. Is it true the autopsy was completed on Friday?"

"Yes. But the family's plan is to have Karen cremated as soon as possible, and then return to Louisiana. I asked Doc to stall for a few days to give us time to investigate and interview the family."

"Understood. But I need to do something to pacify the family, and therefore the mayor. Can you head out to Kahala and make nice with them, get them to lay off for a few days?"

"Now?" I looked at the meat on the counter as I calculated how long it would take me to get to Kahala and back. Less if I could meet Mike and the rest of the ohana in St. Louis Heights.

"That would be appropriate."

"I can leave in about ten minutes," I said.

"Excellent. I'll call the mayor's office and have someone there call the family and let them know to expect you."

"Crap on toast," I said to Mike when I hung up. "I have to run to Kahala. Can you handle the transportation to Haoa's house and I'll meet you all there?"

"Go. My parents will want to drive on their own anyway."

Fortunately I'd already showered and shaved that morning, so all I had to do was pull on a nice aloha shirt and a pair of slacks. I knew the family would probably mistake me once again for a member of the hotel staff, but that was their problem.

I was tempted to put up my flashing light as I drove to Kahala, but traffic wasn't too heavy on the H1 and I made good time. Twenty minutes after leaving my house I was parking in the guest lot at the Albergo.

This time, the door was answered by a handsome young man in his early twenties. "You must be the detective," he said. "I'm David Fontenot."

"Kimo Kanapa'aka," I said, and I shook the hand he stretched out. He seemed like a nice, polite young man. "The family's in the other suite. Come on in for a minute."

I followed him in. The living room was smaller than in the other suite, with doors off to the side for two bedrooms. "This is the one we're sharing with our parents. Aunt Karen and Charles had one bedroom in the other suite, with Grand'Mere in the other bedroom and Uncle Leo bunking on the couch. With Aunt Karen and Charles gone he's been upgraded."

An equally attractive young woman lounged on the sofa, focused on her phone. "This is my sister, Jessica," he said. She and her brother were both wearing bathing suits and with their wet hair, it looked like they'd been pulled in from the beach.

She didn't even look up, but waved in my general direction. "I wanted to ask you something," David said.

"I know this has been a very difficult time for your family and I'm happy to do whatever I can to help."

"Try not to get my dad too agitated, please?" David asked. His eyes turned down, as did the edges of his mouth. "He can get really angry, and then he takes it out on our mother."

"And on us," Jessica said.

"Can I ask how?"

"He doesn't beat us or anything," David said. "Just yells and says mean things. How all the good genetic material in the family tree has run out. Even though I'm getting good grades at Tulane, and I'm the finance manager for my fraternity, he says that I'm a loser."

"And I'm worse," Jessica said. She put down her phone and looked up at me. "That I'm even stupider than Charles and that all I care about is makeup and social media. Which is so not true."

"I know you have access to police records, so I wanted to give you a heads up and explain. My dad has had a couple of arrests back in New Orleans. One was for a bar fight he got into with a bunch of yats."

Jessica saw my confusion. "In New Orleans, a 'yat' is a person who speaks with a blue-collar accent, from the phrase "where y'at?"

I nodded.

"And once someone parked in his spot at his office building, and he bashed the car with a golf club," David said. "He had to take an anger management class and do community service, but it didn't help."

"So please don't agitate him," Jessica said. "For all of us, okay?"

"I'll do my best."

"Let's go, then,' David said, and the three of us walked to the other suite, on the other side of the hallway. This time, at least, Jules Fontenot didn't mistake me for room service. "Detective," he said curtly. "Come in."

Belle reigned, from an armchair that could have come from one of the Doge's palaces. I knew that she was only seventy, but at 75, my mother was much younger and more vibrant. Then again, Belle had suffered the loss of her daughter. But she seemed frail, her arms skinny and mottled.

"When can we get my sister's body and get out of here?" Jules demanded.

Even on vacation, wearing a Brooks Brothers polo and plaid Bermuda shorts, he looked and sounded commanding. I thought he was probably quite a successful lawyer. If he could channel the rage his kids had seen into something positive.

"We are still gathering evidence," I said. "Trying to help the Medical Examiner determine if Karen's death was accidental."

"Of course it was accidental," Leo said. "She was hiking, she fell down a dangerous slope, end of story."

I turned to look at him. He hadn't been getting as much sun as his brother's family, who were all looking nicely tanned. Leo was pale and there were dark circles under his eyes. Was he mourning his sister more than anyone else? Did he have a reason to?"

"I don't understand why we have to leave so quickly, anyway," Jessica said. "I'm just learning to surf. You said we could stay two weeks."

"Your aunt is dead," Belle said sharply. "Have some respect."

"I'm very sorry," I said. "I know how difficult it can be to lose a loved one, and I fully understand your need for closure. But Charles is still recovering in the hospital and until we can talk to him, the ME can't make a definitive decision."

"Charles is useless," Jules said. "You can't believe anything he says."

"For once I agree with my brother," Leo said. "The quicker we get Charles bundled off to a home for disturbed boys the better."

"He's creepy but he's still our cousin," Jessica said. "You can't just give him away like a toy you don't want to play with anymore."

Well, that was nice, to see that someone in this family cared about Charles, if even she did call him creepy.

"The decision of what happens to Charles is mine and mine alone," Belle said. "Karen made that very clear in her will."

"Did her will include information about Charles's father?" I asked.

Belle shook her head. "Karen never mentioned his name."

"So she never told you anything about Omari Fontenot?"

"There's no one named Omari in our family," Jules said, with a sniff.

"I think you'll find that's not correct," I said mildly. "Charles found a family tree online for a different branch of the Fontenot line. One that goes back all the way to slavery. Omari Fontenot is a direct descendant of that line, and before coming to Honolulu Charles was in touch with him, and Omari verified that he and Karen are Charles's parents."

"That's ridiculous!" Leo exploded. "I've never heard of something so unbelievable."

"Believe it," Belle said. "I've known for a long time that there are Black Fontenots out there. I simply didn't know that Karen had been in touch with one."

"Or had sex with him," David said. "That is so gross."

Jessica turned on him. "Why, because he's Black?"

"No, because he's a cousin," David said. "That's incest."

"You are such a dunce. There must be ten generations between them."

"Enough," Belle said. "Whether the boy's father exists is irrelevant to our current situation."

"No, he is quite relevant," I said. "Because Charles contacted him and invited him to Honolulu to meet you all. He's been here since the day after you landed, waiting for Charles to set up a meeting with you."

"Did he kill her?" Leo asked suddenly. "Who knows what Charles has been telling him. God knows he hated all of us and hated living with us. Suppose he told this man that his family is rich, and he'd inherit all his mother's money if Karen died."

"Charles doesn't have any concept of money," David said. "He's always trying to bum cash from me for dumb things like candy bars. Apparently he doesn't even get an allowance."

Belle rapped her cane sharply on the floor. "Where is this man? I want to meet him."

"I can give you his cell phone number," I said.

Jules pulled out his phone. "Give it to me."

I pulled the number from my phone. It felt like I was sending the Biblical Daniel into the lion's den, but I didn't see I had any choice.

"Anyway," I said, after I'd read out the number. I turned to Belle. "You can see why we still have several unanswered questions. I'll make sure that we get in touch with you as soon as your daughter's body can be released."

"Fine," she said, and it was clear I was dismissed.

Chapter 17
Luau

I scrambled back to my SUV and called Mike. "I'm finished here. What's going on?"

"I just got up the hill, and I'll tell you, I am astonished at the platters that have been coming out of the house. Julie and Cathy have been working like mad all morning, recruiting Addie, Owen and Vinnie to chop, stir and roll."

I heard him sniff the air. "I smell lasagna, and there is platter of sushi that looks like the best from a restaurant but was definitely made here. And there's even a chocolate cake and a carrot cake."

Mike must have turned his phone toward the crowd, because I heard Vinnie say, "I peeled the carrots."

Then Owen said he chopped the chocolate, and Addie said, "I helped Mommy roll the sushi." Then they started arguing over who had done more.

Mike put the phone back to his ear. "They make us look like pikers."

"They make us look like men," I said. "And I don't mean that in a positive way."

Since I was coming from Kahala, I swung by Waikiki to pick up my mother. She was already waiting in the lobby of her condo tower for me, and she looked much like the pretty China doll my father had married. She was diminutive but regal, and she glowed with health in a way that was completely different from Belle Charles. My parents had never been as wealthy as the Charles family; my mother had worked hard at my father's construction business, then to raise three strong-willed sons, but you couldn't see any of that struggle in her face or her bearing.

"How are you?" I asked, once I had helped her climb up into the SUV. "You look great."

"Aches and pains," she said. "The price of growing older." She looked over at me when I got behind the steering wheel. "And you?"

"I'm good." I told her about Ray and Julie returning to Honolulu, and she nodded approvingly.

"He is very good for you," she said. "Calm. You have always been strong-willed. Mike loves you, so he puts up with you. But Ray helps you balance."

"You are awfully smart, Mom. Tell me what you think of my brothers."

"Lui is like me. Very determined. You know how poor my parents were when I was growing up. I knew it was up to me to make a better life for my family, and I did. Lui is as forceful as you are, but more directed. And Liliha is very much like me. From a poor family and determined to live well."

I couldn't argue with that. "And Haoa?"

"Haoa is a throwback to a previous generation," she said. "He is not like your father or me, though I see bits of both of us in him. He is so connected to the land, but sometimes he focuses too much on the natural world and not enough on everything else. Tatiana loves him so much, but like Mike with you, she puts up with him. It is good that Keoni will bring some of Lui's energy to Haoa's business."

"You know us all very well."

"I have had many years to observe you. Tell me what you think of your own keikis, what you know so far."

"You know we have never done any testing to determine who the biological father is," I said. "Mike and I both donated sperm. But when we look at them, it's clear that Addie takes after me the most, and Owen is like a miniature Mike."

"And do you love them differently?"

"I couldn't," I said. "They're both my children. I love Addie for what I see in her of me, and I love Owen for what I see of Mike."

"I know you always felt closest to your father," my mother said. "But that doesn't mean I didn't love you as much."

"I miss him," I admitted. "Especially when the keikis do something, and I remember things he said to me, and I wish they could know him."

"Dominic has been good to you," she said. "I see that."

"Yes. It took a long time for us to connect, and he'll never take Dad's place, but I can talk to him."

By the time my mother and I arrived at Haoa and Tatiana's house in St. Louis Heights the party was already rolling. Keola Beamer was playing on the stereo, singing about his whole family rocking in a wooden boat. The keikis were in the pool, laughing and shouting and playing with a huge inflatable swan.

Haoa was at the grill, sweating in an oversized aloha shirt, and Mike was beside him grilling the teriyaki kabobs. I made sure to taste one before anyone else did.

The flavor wasn't as rich or deep as my mother's, but they were good. I put a skewer on a plate and carried it over to where she was sitting with the elegant-as-always Liliha. "Try the teriyaki," I said.

"In a few minutes," my mother said.

"Oh, come on, Mom. Now, please?"

She frowned, but picked up one end of the skewer with her delicately manicured hand, and used her teeth to slide one hunk of beef into her mouth.

She chewed for a moment. "Did you make this?"

"Why? Is it terrible?"

She smiled. "It's not as good as mine. But it's very tasty." She patted my arm. "Don't worry, you have many other talents. You're still a good son."

I kissed her cheek, and it struck me that Charles and Karen Fontenot could never have a moment like that, and it made me sad in the midst of my happiness.

Then I spotted Sergei across the lawn. Talking to Mike.

Did Mike know that I had fooled around with Sergei when we weren't together? I couldn't remember. But I knew Mike didn't care for Tatiana's brother—for one thing, he was bigger than Mike, and at 6'4 with broad shoulders, Mike was accustomed to being the tallest guy in the room, if not always the beefiest.

I could sense trouble brewing so I moved over there as fast as I could without seeming obvious. "Hey, Sergei," I said, sticking out my hand. Instead he grabbed me into a big bear hug.

"Kimo! So great to see you. I've just been talking to your handsome partner here."

"Comparing notes," Mike said.

I raised my eyebrows. "On?" I said, as casually as I could

"Police and fire between here and Anchorage," Mike said. "Sergei is thinking of moving here permanently and joining your force or mine."

"How old are you, Sergei?"

"Aw, gee." He fluttered his hand in front of his face. I stared him down and he said, "Thirty-eight."

"Too old for Federal law enforcement," I said.

"I was just telling Sergei that we prefer new fire recruits no older than twenty-eight to thirty," Mike said. "Which leaves him with your department."

Oh, God. The thought of Sergei Baranov as a cop made me shudder. He was certainly smart enough and fit enough. It was his judgment that I worried about. During his previous stay with his sister, he'd stripped and performed sex acts on video, and managed to put Haoa's business at risk by hiring undocumented workers.

"Unless you have any better ideas," Sergei said. "I'm fed up with

Unruly Son

Alaskan winters, and even the summers aren't warm enough for me. My mom wanted to come down and visit Tatiana, and I volunteered to escort her."

He nodded toward one side of the room, where my sister-in-law Tatiana, a golden-haired beauty with an effusive laugh, stood beside a woman nearly her height with iron-gray hair and a scowl on her face. She didn't look like she needed escorting. So she probably wanted Sergei out of Alaska as much as he wanted to go.

"So, Kimo, any ideas?" Sergei asked.

"You like to work outside, don't you?" I asked. He'd been happy at Haoa's landscaping business until he screwed up.

"I do."

"And I know you're good with people. Charming."

"Aw, shucks."

Mike was glaring at me, but I ignored him. "Have you thought about being a park ranger?" I asked. "That's kind of like law enforcement, and a lot of it is outdoors, and working with people. We have four national parks and one national historic trail. You have some college behind you, don't you?"

"I have an AA in Alaska Native Studies. I did some park work when I was younger."

"There you go. You've got a good start."

"Thanks, Kimo. Maybe I can finally do something to make my mother proud of me." He grimaced. "And get my siblings off my back."

His mother motioned him over, and he headed in her direction.

Sergei had been almost as much trouble to his parents as Charles had been to Karen. And yet his family had rallied around him, time and again, no matter how unruly he had become. And when his sister married my brother, he had joined our ohana along with her, and he had become like family. Though I was sure there were times when Haoa would have liked to push Sergei off a cliff, he hadn't.

"Did you and Sergei really..." Mike began.

"Yes. I never said I was a virgin when I met you." I smiled at him. "And you know the kind of men who attract me."

"I used to assume that was smart guys," he said.

"Sergei is smart when he wants to be. And he has a big..."

"Not bigger than mine." Mike put his hands on his waist.

"Honestly? It was one night, eleven years ago. You really want me to remember the details? Or I could just pull him inside and do a quick measure. You up for that?"

"Not with his mother here, and your mother, and mine." He leaned down and whispered something in my ear that made me blush.

Chapter 18
Cui Bono

Monday morning, Ray and I were at our desks at eight, and Sampson called us into his office a few minutes later. "The mayor called me at home last night to ask about the progress of our investigation and I had to tell him that we were letting the family grieve and allowing the boy time to recover. He was sympathetic but he still wants this case wrapped up as soon as possible. We need to understand what happened to Karen and Charles Fontenot up on that mountain and ensure that there were no outside actors involved."

"Ray and I were out at Hanauma Bay on Saturday with our families, and we spoke to a woman who witnessed Charles be violent toward his mother. I spoke with a clerk at the Albergo who saw Charles have a tantrum. I've communicated with Doc Takayama, and he's willing to hold Karen's body until we've had a chance to interview the family."

"Good start. Keep me in the loop."

Thus dismissed, we went back to our desks.

"I've been thinking, and while all the evidence we have so far, including the ME's report, indicates that Karen Fontenot's death might be a terrible, unfortunate accident," Ray said, as he sat down. "But suppose we look at it from a different angle."

"You mean as a deliberate homicide?"

"Exactly. And what's one of the first questions we ask in a homicide?"

"Cui bono?"

"Yup. Who benefits from Karen's death?"

"My first impression of the Fontenot family, based on that one quick visit and the fact that they were staying at a luxury resort, was that they are well-heeled. But Gunter has a friend who works there, and he relayed to me that Belle Fontenot's credit card had been overstretched, and that her son had to provide a new one."

"It happens," Ray said. "My uncle started to get forgetful a couple of years ago. He'd get a bill in, file it away without paying it. My aunt blew up when her credit card was denied at Macy's when she was trying to buy new bed linens."

"So it could be a simple mistake," I said. "When I've met with them, they have all looked rich, from clothes to shoes to watches and jewelry."

"I'll give you my opinion when we're finished."

"Why don't we divide and conquer," I said. "I'll take on Belle and Emeline Fontenot and you take the brothers."

We each turned to our computers and started digging. We finished about the same time, and I volunteered to start because Belle was the oldest. "Belle Charles was born in 1949 at Charity Hospital in New Orleans. She had a younger brother named Henri Charles, born in 1951, who died in Vietnam in 1971 and was, interestingly, buried in the military cemetery at Punchbowl."

"You think that's why the family came to Honolulu?" Ray asked.

"Possibly. Belle is what, seventy years old? Maybe she wanted to visit her brother's grave while she could still travel."

I looked back at my notes. "In 1970 she married a man named Louis Fontenot at his family plantation, Belle Terre. From what I can tell, Louis managed the property and the family assets. I found some real estate transactions from the 1990s as the family sold off chunks of their land. For the most part, Belle was a society wife. Louis died in 2010, and after that it looks like she stopped going out."

Ray said, "Jules Fontenot graduated from Tulane and its law school. He's a name partner in the law firm of Hodges, Alphonse, Britain and Fontenot, with offices on Canal Street. I took a quick look at their website. They focus on corporate clients, and Jules's specialty is real estate law."

"Sounds lucrative," I said.

"He married Emeline Alphonse—probably the boss's daughter—in 1996, and they have two children. David is twenty, and Jessica is eighteen. Jules and Emeline own a home on Coliseum Street in an area of New Orleans called the Garden District."

He popped up a picture on his screen. "Zillow says it's a four-bedroom, three-bath home in a vaguely Federal style, with arched windows, a second-floor balcony over the whole front of the house, and a peaked roof. Valued it at $1.2 million."

"So he has done well for himself," I said.

"Unlike his younger brother," Ray said. "Leo Fontenot's Facebook page says he's a graduate of Tulane, like his brother, but didn't go to law school. Six years ago, he registered a "life event" – his marriage to Rebecca Nguyen, who worked at the Beauty Nails salon on St. Ann Street in the French Quarter."

He flipped to another screen. "Only a single picture, which looks like it was taken at some government office. Three years later he changed his status to single. He 'liked' the Tulane Green Wave football team, Walk-On's Sports Bistreaux, and Sports Radio ESPN 1420." Ray looked up. "That's it for social media. So I jumped back to real estate records. He and Rebecca co-owned an apartment near his brother's home, but that was sold in 2011, about the same time that his status on Facebook changed."

"He's currently still single?" I asked.

Ray nodded. "And it doesn't appear that he's gainfully employed, either. I couldn't find any record of a job, and I found a series of addresses where he had resided for one year or less, probably rentals. His most current address is a studio in the French Quarter." He looked back at me. "Not a cheap place-- rents are close to a thousand dollars a month."

"So how's he supporting himself? Stealing change from his mother's pocketbook?"

"He'd have to have pretty grabby fingers. What did you find on Karen?"

"She was born in 1976 at the same hospital where her mother was born. She followed Jules and Leo to Tulane, and then law school. She joined the district attorney's office in New Orleans and worked there for three years, then joined a law firm in the city as a criminal attorney. Charles was born in 2004, and in 2006 she left the firm."

I looked up from my screen. "There's no indication that she set up her own practice. It looks like she is living with her mother and looking after Charles full-time."

"I can imagine he takes a lot of looking after," Ray said. "Vinnie is a pretty normal kid and there's two of us, and he runs us ragged sometimes."

"I can't tell if he's being home-schooled or not," I said. "But the family should be able to say. I'm just not ready to talk to them yet. How do you feel about taking a look at the crime scene?"

"Sounds like fun."

I shook my head. "Spoken like a true homicide detective."

Chapter 19
Talk Story

"We'll have to make a pit stop at Aeia Heights on the way. You'll want long pants and a long-sleeved shirt, and whatever kind of boots you have for getting through mud and maybe some mild climbing. And bug spray."

I dropped him off, then dressed the way I'd told him to, in a pair of jeans, heavy socks and hiking boots, with a long-sleeved microfiber fisherman's shirt. I added a broad-brimmed hat, to protect myself from the sun.

When I drove back up the hill, I was pleased to see he'd dressed almost the same way. "Great minds think alike, brah," I said. "This is going to be just like old times."

"Let's hope I don't regret this decision to come back to Hawai'i before the day is out," he said, but I could tell from his tone that he was excited to get back to work.

As we drove to Wa'ahila Ridge, I told him everything Doc Takayama had said. "We're going to look for anything that pushes his decision one way or the other?" he asked.

"Exactly." It felt so good to be with a partner again, especially one who thought the same way I did.

"And why do we think we'll find something the crime scene techs didn't?"

Oh. Ray had the habit of deflating my ideas as often as going along with them.

I thought about that for a minute, as I steered us off the H1 at the 6th Avenue exit. "They were looking for evidence," I said finally. "We're going to use that evidence to tell a story, if that makes sense. Talk story, as the Hawaiians say."

He nodded. "It does. But if you push me down that ravine in the name of storytelling I won't be happy."

"I guarantee you I have no interest in killing you as soon as you start back to work. I doubt you're even qualified for workmen's comp at this point."

"Then I'll be the one doing the pushing."

We parked in the lot and started climbing. The park personnel had taken down the crime scene tape, but they had put up a temporary barrier to keep people from falling the same way Karen Fontenot had. We reached the point and stopped there.

"What does ironwood look like?" Ray asked.

I pointed to the leafy pine-like tree ahead of us. "That's ironwood. Very strong, hence the name. I don't think anyone could have broken a branch off to use as a weapon. Have to be something found nearby."

I had remembered a number of branches in the area, the result of a lightning strike, but they'd all been taken away by the crime scene investigators.

The woods around us were gloomy and only narrow rays of light filtered down from the canopy. I heard the song of a bird, and some rustling in the underbrush. Wild boar sometimes got up there, as well as invasive iguanas.

"We're at a wide spot along the trail, and up ahead I see two different paths to take," Ray said. "This would be a good spot to stop and look at the map."

"I agree." I pulled my copy of the trail map out of my pocket and looked down at it.

"I'm talking more about Karen Fontenot than us. While her attention was on the map, she could have taken a few steps to the right. Maybe angling for better light. It's pretty dark in here."

"That would open the possibility that she stepped too close to the edge, lost her balance, and went down."

Ray nodded. "Was there a map anywhere near her?"

"We'll have to check the CSI report back at the office. If she had the map open, there's an opportunity for someone to come up behind her and whack her on the side of the head with a piece of ironwood," I said.

Ray leaned down and felt the ground. "It's soft and damp. No hard leaves to crunch."

"So she might not hear someone who came up behind her."

"A stranger, or her son," Ray said. "I know you haven't been able to talk to him, but where do you think he fits in all this? Is he the assailant? Was he standing nearby when his mother fell? Or something in between?"

"From what I understand, he's a strong-willed boy, and he and his mother liked to hike together. Or at least she liked to take him on hikes, because he likes trees and leaves and rocks. I could see him going ahead along the trail while she stops to look at the map. Or maybe he lingered behind, fascinated by something."

"He sounds like the key. Any idea when he'll be ready to talk?"

"We need to ask again."

We climbed up the trail a few feet, walked around, peered at scuff marks in the ground. But none of it gave us anything new, and it became increasingly clear that we needed to speak to Charles Fontenot.

We had both shut down our cell phones when we got to the park, because there was little reception up there on the mountain, and when we turned them on again, I had a message. "You know area code 504?" I asked.

"New Orleans," he said. "Years ago, between the time of caller ID and everyone having a cell phone, I learned the area codes for major cities."

"Really? Boston."

"617."

"San Francisco."

"415."

"I have no idea if you're right or not, but I'm impressed." I called the number back.

"This is Jules Fontenot. When can we have my sister's body released? My mother wanted her buried near my uncle Henri in Punchbowl, but they've told us that's not allowed, so we want to have her cremated. My mother will take custody of her remains to be interred in the family crypt in New Orleans."

"I'm afraid it's not that simple. It's my job to investigate your sister's death and help the Medical Examiner come to a cause of death before he can release the body."

"What is there to investigate? She fell down a hill and died."

"If that's the case, I'll work with the ME to establish that."

"This is a ridiculous situation," Jules said. I heard him speak off the phone to someone, possibly his mother. When he came back to me all he said was, "We'll have our attorney make some calls."

Then he hung up.

Chapter 20
Call and Answer

I dropped Ray at the Alapai Headquarters for his last meeting with HR, but I was too restless to sit at my desk. I decided I'd head over to the Queen's Medical Center and see if Charles Fontenot was talking yet. I had to cool my heels in a waiting room for nearly half an hour before I could get to talk to the psychologist who was supervising Charles Fontenot. At least she was apologetic.

She was a frizzy-haired haole woman who spoke with the broad accent of the American Midwest. "I'm Dr. Leenie," she said. "How can I help you?"

I showed her my badge and explained that I was investigating Karen Fontenot's death. "The key in understanding what happened to her is going to be speaking with her son. When can I do that?"

"He's physically sound, and we have no reason to keep him here other than the fact that his family don't want him with them and haven't told us what they want to do with him."

My mouth dropped open, and Dr. Leenie nodded.

"Not the best family environment to release a traumatized young man into."

"You said he's physically sound. What about mentally? Is he speaking?"

"Barely. He says no a lot. Not happy with the food choices, apparently, and he doesn't like having a police officer outside his room preventing him from leaving. Is that your department policy?"

"Right now we don't know if Charles killed his mother, which would make him a suspect. Or if someone else killed his mother and would like to remove him from the picture, which would mean he needs police protection."

"Either way, he's going to have to leave soon. We can't keep patients here indefinitely if there's nothing we can do for them."

"Can I speak to him?"

"That depends. Are you interrogating him as a suspect? In that case he needs a parent or guardian present. If no one in his family is willing to serve in that case, then we'd have to get someone from social services involved."

"What about if I'm talking to him as a witness?"

She sighed. "My understanding is that police can interview a minor alone in such a case."

"That's my understanding, too," I said and stood up. "Can I see him?"

Dr. Leenie led me to an elevator, down to the ground floor, and through a maze of hallways to another building. I stopped at the snack shop. "I've been told that it's good to approach a kid like Charles with food. Any idea what he likes?"

"So far the only thing he's accepted without complaint has been chocolate pudding."

I bought a variety of candy bars as well as a bottle of passion fruit, orange and guava juice, known colloquially in the islands as pog. If he didn't like it I'd drink it myself.

We rode up in another elevator. I saw Jeremy Hoult on a chair outside a room down the hall from us. "I can take it from here," I said.

"You don't want me to come in with you?"

"Maybe later, if I can't get him to talk." I held up the candy bars. "But I'll see what Mr. Hershey and Mr. Mars can do for me first."

I greeted Jeremy at the door, then nodded toward Charles. "How's he doing?"

"Not a happy camper. Pretty much throws a tantrum at everyone who goes inside."

Good to know. Charles had a single room, painted a light green that was supposed to be soothing to patients. A print of Diamond Head hung across from his hospital bed. He was reclining there, playing a video game on a hand-held unit.

The door to the closet was open, and I saw a suitcase at the bottom, with a row of clothes hanging above it, though he was still in a hospital gown. Someone had come to visit him, to bring him his stuff. Because they wanted him to feel more comfortable?

Or because he wasn't going home with them?

He looked older than I'd expected, though I guessed that was what fourteen looked like. An unruly mop of dark hair, an acne pimple on one cheek. His skin was a warm tan, much like his father's. The gown made him look thinner and more fragile than he probably was.

"Charles?" I asked.

He didn't look up from his game. As I got closer I heard the rhythmic pop-pop-pop of handguns and the rapid bangs of fire, accompanied by the squeal of brakes.

I pulled a chair up next to his bed and laid out the candy bars on his bedside table. Then I sat down.

He reached for one of the candy bars and I held onto the other end. "Not until you look at me," I said.

He shut the game off and looked at me. I smiled and nodded my head. "You can have the candy bar now."

He took it and meticulously began peeling the wrapper back, eating the bar in small bites from one end.

"My name's Kimo, and I'm a police officer."

He nodded slightly but wouldn't make eye contact.

"I'm real sorry about what happened to your mom. I grew up

right near those woods and my friends and I use to roam about all through there."

"I collect leaves," he said, his focus still on the candy bar.

"I used to do that, too," I said. "I'd dry them between pieces of newspaper."

"They lose their color that way," he said.

"Really? How do you do it?"

He finally looked up at me. "You need wax paper and an iron. When I was little my mother used to do the ironing for me but then she let me do it. You put an old towel on your ironing board and then a layer of wax paper like you get at the grocery store. You have grocery stores here in Hawai'i, don't you?"

"We sure do. I bet I even have some wax paper in my cabinet."

"Then you can do it. You put your leaves down on top of the wax paper, and then you put another layer of paper down. Then you iron them. It's quicker than waiting for them to dry out and you can do a lot of different leaves at once. We didn't bring an iron with us to Hawai'i, but they had one in the hotel room. We got leaves from every park we went to and we ironed them."

"I'll have to remember that. I have two kids, a boy and a girl, and I'll bet they'd like to iron leaves like that."

He finished his candy bar and looked at the array on the table. "Can I have another?"

"Sure. What kind do you like?"

"I like the ones with nuts." He picked a second candy bar and started peeling away the wrapper as he'd done with the first.

"Were you with your mother when she fell, or were you collecting leaves?"

"We didn't always stay together, but I was supposed to stay within the sound of her voice," he said. "Sometimes I get distracted by things I find."

"And that day?"

"I went up the trail a few feet. But I heard her when she yelled."

"Did she yell for you?"

He shook his head. "It was more like one of those Tarzan yells." He imitated. "Ah-wow-wow," his voice diminishing at the end.

"I'd be scared to hear that in the woods. Were you scared?"

He looked at me like I'd used a word he didn't understand. "I went back down the trail to where she was but she wasn't there anymore."

His finger got caught in the candy bar wrapper and he tore at it. "I looked all around and I called for her and she didn't answer. That wasn't right. She promised me she would always answer me when I called her."

I imagined the scene for myself. Charles standing in that clearing, calling for his mother, and her not answering. Because she couldn't.

"Then what did you do?"

"I kept looking. I went up the trail and down the trail and then I got lost from the trail and I kept calling for her and she didn't answer. Why didn't she answer?"

"You know why, Charles," I said gently.

"Because she was dead." He pulled the last chunk of chocolate out of the wrapper and threw the wrapper away. Because it was so light, it didn't have the effect he expected.

"My mother wanted me to go to Boy Scouts when I was little," he said. "So I could go on nature hikes with them. She bought me the outfit and took me to the school where they were meeting." He looked up at me. "But I punched a boy in the eye because he called me weird, and then I couldn't go on hikes with them. So my mother took me."

I nodded.

"But she always answered when I called for her, even when we were in swamps or woods. But this time she didn't answer. I called and called until my throat was hoarse."

My heart was breaking for him. I could imagine promising the same thing to Addie and Owen, that I'd always answer when they called for me. And then what if one day I couldn't answer anymore?

Charles started banging his head on the wall behind him, and a moment later a pair of nurses rushed in. "You'll have to leave," one of them said to me, and I stood up and backed away.

They grabbed him by his arms and spoke to him quietly, but he wouldn't stop banging. I walked out as they were tying his arms down to the bed.

Chapter 21
Rashomon

I was really shaken by my visit with Charles Fontenot. Maybe I should have taken Ray or Dr. Leenie with me. Maybe I shouldn't have pressed him so hard, made him relive the moment when he realized his mother was never going to answer him.

But I had to know what happened, didn't I? I was still that impulsive kid in high school, who needed to be restrained by Harry and Terri to keep me from doing dumb things.

I walked numbly out of the hospital and then down the street to a Kope Bean, where I managed to order myself a longboard raspberry mocha and then sit in a back corner of the coffee shop. Since I didn't have my iPad with me, I pulled out a pocket notebook to record my interview with Charles. But it was hard to figure out what to write, beyond the specifics of which candy bar he ate, and the words he said. What did they mean?

In our junior year at Punahou, Harry, Terri and I took Asian History from Mrs. Kita. I remember one dismal rainy week when she showed us the movie *Rashomon* over several days. I was fascinated by Kurosawa's approach, showing us the same incident over and over again, from different points of view.

It was a film that kept resonating with me the longer I stayed a cop. I learned not to believe everything a witness said, because any two people who saw the same event saw it differently and remembered it differently.

I had run across witnesses who had photographic memories, and recorded every detail they saw, and still missed things out of their frame of reference. And I had met witnesses who were so traumatized by what they saw that their brains shut down, and they deliberately blocked everything.

Most people, of course, were somewhere in the middle. I remembered a man who insisted the woman he'd seen running from the robbery of a bank wore a red dress. He was so sure of that, and yet the detail didn't fit. The woman we had arrested wore a purple dress with a scooped neck and a pleated skirt.

It took a lot of questioning for the witness to realize that his wife had a dress just like the one he'd seen on the robber, with a similar neck and skirt. His wife's was red, so he had applied that detail to what he'd witnessed.

When I thought back over what Charles Fontenot had said. He had never stated, or denied, that he had pushed his mother into the ravine. He had made a series of short statements that easily could have camouflaged the part of the scene that upset him most.

It did explain why we hadn't found him near his mother. He was distressed and thought she was still alive and not answering him, so he had continued to range around the forest until he was found.

I was obsessing over what Charles had said when Ray called. "I had some more paperwork to finish and I'm heading down to the armorer to get issued my weapon. Where are you?"

"Kope Bean near the hospital."

"You didn't go see Charles alone, did you? I thought you were supposed to wait for me."

I sighed deeply. "I know, but after talking to his uncle this morning I just wanted to get this investigation finished. Charles said a few things, but I don't know what I learned."

"Come pick me up and we'll talk it through."

Unruly Son

That was what I had missed in not having a regular partner. I had worked on a couple of cases with a rookie FBI agent, and he'd been a good sounding board, as well as having some skills of his own that complemented mine. But in the end he was a government number cruncher and not a street-smart detective.

And that was what I had in Ray Donne.

It was the end of our shift, so I drove us homeward. On the way back to Aiea Heights, we talked through my meeting with Charles. "I used the technique you told me about. Brought him candy. We started talking about collecting leaves, and I segued into that morning with his mother."

"How?"

I tried to remember. "I asked him if he was with his mother when she fell."

"Just like that?"

"Well, I asked if he was off finding leaves, or if he was with her."

"Still. That's a pretty abrupt transition."

"What would you have done?"

He shrugged. "Hard to say when you're not there. But maybe started out that morning. What did they have for breakfast? Was he excited about the hike? Was there a reason why she picked that park that day?"

"You can ask those questions tomorrow." I told him how someone had brought all his stuff to the hospital. "I don't think they want to take him back to New Orleans."

"They have to, Kimo. That's his grandmother there in the hotel."

"And maybe they think Charles killed his mother. If in a few years, Vinnie killed you, even accidentally, you think your mother would be happy to take him in?"

"You can't make that kind of comparison."

"Let's look at Belle Fontenot," I said, as we inched forward in rush hour traffic. "She has three children. Karen is the baby of the family, the only girl. Like her oldest brother Jules, she did what was expected of her for years—college, law school, good job. Then she veered off the path, having an illegitimate child. But still, the baby gets away with a lot of stuff without losing the parents' love."

"Okay, I get that. Belle loves Karen."

"Then we bring Charles into the mix. Charles is disturbed, by any measure. He's the reason why Karen has to give up her job. Belle can't brag about her daughter anymore. She can't even brag about her grandson, because anybody who meets him figures out quickly there's something wrong with him."

"Does that matter?"

"I had a friend from New Orleans at UC Santa Cruz. She was raised a lot like Karen was, an old New Orleans family with money. She had a debutante ball. Her father's best friend was the president of Rex, which made him the King of Mardi Gras. She used to go over to this girl's house to watch the parade go by."

"So?"

"So that kind of social position is important to people like Belle Fontenot. She had Karen on the right track until Charles showed up. I'd imagine she could make some excuse for the illegitimate birth. People would talk, but these days everybody's family has things like that."

I paused, thinking of how I wanted to say this. I hadn't worked with Ray for a couple of years, and I didn't want him to think I'd become prejudiced in his absence—or more prejudiced, because no matter how liberal and open you are, you still have some vestige of prejudice in you, from the way you were brought up, or a person you encountered along the way, or your interpretation of history.

"There's the additional complication that Omari Fontenot is Black, and a descendant of a slave and a rapist."

A car tried to nose in front of me and I blew my horn angrily.

"Calm down, Kimo. Charles's father is Black. What does that say about your theory of Karen being a favorite child?"

I took a deep breath, kept my foot on the brake, and let the car move in front of me. The man at the wheel waved politely, and I waved back.

"You're more the psychologist than I am. Talk to me about displacement."

He turned to look at me and quirked up the corner of his mouth. He didn't say anything at first. "So. Displacement. I'm assuming you mean that Belle is angry at Karen for having a Black child. But Karen is her baby, doing everything right until Charles comes along. So instead of getting angry at Karen, she shifts her anger to Charles."

"Exactly. Add to that Charles's behavioral problems, and even though he's her grandson, I can see Belle hating him."

Ray nodded. "And now, if you consider that maybe Charles killed her baby girl, Belle can't stand to have him around anymore."

"This is all a great theory, but it doesn't lead us anywhere in figuring out who killed Karen, or if she lost her balance and fell."

"But it does give us some insight into family dynamics. Where do the brothers fit in?"

"I'm not sure I can give a dispassionate opinion on that, because I have two older brothers myself and they used to gang up on me when I was a kid. I came up with a million reasons why as I got older, even down to given names."

"Names?"

"You know my oldest brother, Lui. That's his Hawaiian name, but it's not on his birth certificate. Louis John Kanapa'aka. Then Haoa, same deal. Howard Charles Kanapa'aka."

"Okay."

"Then me. Kimo James Kanapa'aka."

He nodded. "So you're the only one with a legal Hawaiian name."

"And since Kimo is Hawaiian for James, it's like I have the same name twice. I used to obsess over that."

"The things kids worry about. Last year Vinnie asked how come his grandma calls him Vincenzo, which was her brother's name, but his name is Vincent. We had this convoluted conversation about the Americanization of names. How when my great-grandfather came to the United States he changed our name from Donatello to Donne to avoid prejudice."

I finally got off the H1 and the traffic eased. "But to get back to the point, we don't know how Jules and Leo treated Charles. From the way that someone dropped his stuff at the hospital, I think they're not too happy to have a mixed-race nephew, especially not one with behavioral problems."

"Who might have killed their sister." Ray turned to me again. "But this still isn't our problem. It's not up to us to decide what happens to Charles Fontenot if he's not guilty."

"But what if he is?"

Chapter 22
Downhill

I dropped Ray at Sandra and Cathy's and went home. Throughout dinner, I was distracted, wondering about Charles Fontenot. Had I done the wrong thing in going to see him on my own? Would that set back the investigation? What was he eating for dinner—hospital food, while his relatives were dining out at the Albergo's gourmet restaurant?

"You're in another world," Mike said, as we finished eating. "Thinking about your case?"

"The whole case revolves around this poor kid, and no matter what I find out things aren't going to come out well for him."

"You know that it's not your job to wave a magic wand and create a happy ending for him, don't you?"

"I know. But sometimes I wish this was the end of *Peter Pan*, and if we all clap really hard fairies will have magic powers."

He snorted with laughter. "I think that comes more toward the middle. At the end Wendy takes all the boys except Peter back to London."

"What if his family doesn't want to take Charles back to New Orleans with them?"

"Then Social Services steps in," Mike said, as he began ferrying our dirty plates to the dishwasher. "Somebody with experience at this talks to Charles and the rest of his family and finds the best place for him. They have money, don't they?"

"I'm not sure. Gunter's friend said the grandmother's credit card was denied."

"Still, chances are he won't end up in a hellhole. He'll go to one of those places where rich kids with behavior problems go to get sorted."

"What if they won't pay? Or they can't?"

"Kimo. This is not your problem. And didn't you say his mother was a lawyer? And she was obsessed with taking care of him?"

"Yeah."

"I wouldn't be surprised if she had some clause in her will regarding him. Her money to be put toward his care. She might even have a facility already picked out."

I felt better after that. From everything I'd heard, Karen Fontenot was a smart, wealthy, protective single mother. She must have provided for Charles in her will.

I wanted to go up the street to see Addie and Owen, to reassure myself that they were all right, but I resisted. I didn't want to transfer my neuroses to them.

Tuesday morning Ray and I were about to start brainstorming when Sampson called us in to his office.

"You went to see the boy yesterday," he said to me.

"Charles Fontenot. Yes."

"Even though I told you specifically that I wanted you to focus on the other angle, that this was a random killing. That Donne was supposed to look into the family."

I didn't understand why Sampson was angry. "I checked with missing persons. No one reported missing in any parks on O'ahu over the last year. No homicides committed in or near any park during that period, except for a domestic. Since Ray was doing more paperwork, I jumped in to look at what you assigned to him." I looked at him. "Is there a problem?"

"Did you know that the nurses at Queen's have to document any time they use restraints on a patient?"

I shook my head, though I was beginning to understand his anger.

"They do. When a nurse entered the reason for the use of restraints on Charles Fontenot yesterday, she cited your visit. That ramped up to the nursing supervisor, and then to the hospital administrator. He complained to the chief of police."

He glared at us. "Shit rolls downhill, gentleman. When the chief complains to me about the behavior of one of my detectives, I nimbly jump out of the way and let it continue to roll down and splatter all over you."

I resisted the urge to wipe my face, which was a good idea.

"Consider yourselves splattered. Not a good way to start your return, Donne. Keep an eye on your partner, please."

"Will do, sir."

"You can go." We stood up to leave, and he added, "Welcome back, Ray. You've been missed."

"Aw, that was sweet," I said when we got back to our desks. "You've been missed."

"Sweet except for the 'you got me covered in shit on my return' part." He sat at his desk, tested out his chair. "I want to talk to the family myself, but because you've had first contact you should come along with me. And I want to talk to Charles, too, but I'm going to have to wait until after I speak to the family."

"Something interesting," I said. "The complaint about me came up through hospital channels. Not from anyone in Charles's family."

"You really think they don't care about him anymore," Ray said. "That's something I'll have to ask about."

I put together all the material I had collected on the family and shared it with Ray through the police computer system. While he read, I went back to the records on missing persons and homicides, and double and triple-checked to be sure I hadn't missed anything. No unsolved homicides in a public park, no one gone missing who didn't have a reason to disappear. No tourists missing, either.

"Is this all you have on the family?"

I turned to Ray.

He leaned back in his chair. "It seems that we have two options here. First, Karen fell down that slope on her own. Death by misadventure. Doc's report will support that."

"I agree. But his report can equally support someone hitting her and knocking her down, or simply pushing her in a way that led to her falling down the slope."

"That's correct. Which leads us to option two. Karen was killed by person or persons unknown. That could lead in any of three directions."

He grabbed a pad from his desk and started drawing. The first line split into two. The left arrow pointed to *death by misadventure*. The right arrow read *homicide*.

Then he drew three lines downward from the word homicide. The left-most read *random stranger*.

"Because I didn't discover Karen Fontenot's body until at least two days after she went down that ravine," I said, "the area where she stood before going down was compromised by many tourists going up and down the path. Crime scene didn't find anything that would lead us to any specific individual."

Ray said, "If our killer is a random stranger, there's very little chance we'll find him or her. There won't be any connections to Karen other than time and place."

"I agree. The only way we'd get a break is if the killer kills again and leaves us a clue to follow."

The second arrow he drew ended with the words motivated stranger. "What do we know about Karen's character?" he asked.

"Smart. Privileged background. Trained as an attorney. Dedicated mom. Under a lot of stress because of her son."

"Because she was stressed, it's possible she pissed someone off along the way to the park, right? Gave the wrong person the finger on the road. Took someone's parking space at the park."

"So that's what you mean by motivated stranger."

"Exactly. We need to trace Karen's movements from the time she left the hotel to the time she arrived at the park."

I held up my index finger. "Problem. The only person who can tell us that is Charles, and he's not exactly talkative."

"Not to you. But I'll give it a try."

"What about your third arrow?"

"That's our limited pool of suspects." He wrote the names Belle, Jules and Leo, then added Jules's wife Emeline and their children David and Jessica. "We need to interview each one of the family members and verify their alibis. Did any of them have a motive to kill Karen?"

"There are three elements, my friend," I said. "Means, motive, and opportunity. The biggest problem with these folks is going to be means. Karen drove to the park from the hotel in Kahala with Charles."

"Didn't you say that they had two rental cars?"

"Yes. But they originally said that Karen's car was gone, and it wasn't until the next day that they notified us that she'd taken the car registered in her brother's name instead."

"Accidentally? Or deliberately? Did anyone fingerprint the car?"

"I don't know. I don't know what happened to the car after I discovered Karen's body."

"You work on that and I'll do some digging on the family."

I didn't want to bother the family, so I called the rental car company. After quite a while on hold, a manager came on the line. "This is Beyonce, how may I help you?" she said, with a musical accent. So much for Hawaiian names when there were charismatic musicians out there.

I introduced myself. "I'm trying to find out what happened to one of your cars." I read her the license plate number. "Did you pick it up from Wa'ahila Ridge?"

"Oh, this is about that poor dead woman. Let me check." I heard her tapping keys. "That car was rented in the name of Jules Fontenot," she said, though she pronounced it fon-te-knot. "I have a note here in the system that Mr. Fontenot had a discussion with another manager. He had another car, in his sister's name, at the Albergo d'Italia hotel in Kahala. He wanted us to switch the contract so that the car there would be in his name."

"And did you do that?"

"We can't. Any change in the car rental agreement has to be initiated in person. Then he asked us to pick up the car at Wa'ahila Ridge and bring it to Kahala and take away the car in his sister's name."

"Did you do that?"

"Apparently the other manager notified him that he would need a death certificate to return the car in his sister's name."

I knew that he didn't have that certificate, because Doc Takayama hadn't issued one. "Ouch. I can bet he wasn't happy about that."

"Apparently he cursed the manager and hung up, after threatening to call our corporate office and register a complaint."

"Did he do that?"

"There's no record here. But off the record, the call lines to corporate have a very heavy wait time right now. Well, always. But we're not supposed to tell customers that."

"Where's the car?"

"The car in Karen Fontenot's name was dropped off at our airport location on Friday. We don't require ID to return a car. You just pull up in line and leave the key in the ignition. The attendant checks for damage, and if there isn't any, the attendant issues a receipt. Ninety-five percent of customers proceed to the shuttle van."

I thought about that for a minute. If Jules Fontenot returned Karen's car, he had to have help. Someone to drive him to Wa'ahila Ridge, follow him to the airport, then drive him back to Kahala. His kids were both old enough to drive, or he could have recruited his brother Leo. Belle appeared to be too old and fragile to be trusted with a rental car in an unfamiliar city.

"What happens if someone rents a car from you, then comes back to the lot, but doesn't want to return the car. Do you keep records of cars coming in and out?"

"Not coming in, but going out."

"Can you check on the other car, the one registered to Jules Fontenot? Did it enter your lot around the same time the other car was returned?"

I heard her tapping keys again. "Yes. About five minutes after Karen's car was returned."

"And just to clarify, a car is cleaned after it's returned?"

"Oh, yes, we do a very thorough cleaning."

"And this car, is it still on your lot? Or has it been rented since?"

More tapping. "It came in on Friday morning and went out on Friday afternoon. Then it was returned Sunday evening and went out again yesterday morning."

I thanked her and hung up. Online, though, I discovered that her company had been cited several times for delivering cars to new customers that hadn't been cleaned properly. Even so, it was doubtful that after two more renters, any useful fingerprints would remain. And what would they tell us, anyway? No matter which family member's prints were on the steering wheel, there was nothing to say when they had gotten there.

I opened a new computer document and entered all the details I had of the movements of the two rental cars. There was still a big hole, though. We had only Jules Fontenot's word that no one had noticed Karen had taken the car registered to Jules until the day after she went missing.

What if one of them had taken that car out, followed Karen to the mountains, then waited for Charles to wander off before confronting her?

That would mean one of her family members had to have a motive, which sent me back to square one.

Chapter 23
Tumble

Ray turned to me after he finished his call. "Well, you made an impression on Charles."

"Look, I know I was wrong. I'm sorry if it makes extra work for you to clean up after me."

"I didn't say it was a bad impression. He's asked the nurses several times when the candy man is coming back."

"Oh."

"Yeah, oh. The nurse I spoke to says he's most communicative in the afternoon. Apparently his mother got him hooked on some kind of New Orleans coffee first thing, so it takes him a while to wake up without it."

"Café du Monde," I said. "New Orleans legend. They make their own blend of coffee with chicory in it." I shrugged. "Though I don't know what chicory is."

I turned to my computer and did a quick search. "Cool. You roast the root of the endive plant and then grind it up. That's called chicory, and in New Orleans they mix it together and serve it like café au lait, with lots of milk."

"Excellent information, Sherlock. But sadly we are not in New Orleans."

"We may not be in New Orleans, but we can still buy the ground coffee at Big Mo's Excellent Java Joint, brew it up ourselves and pour it into a thermos for delivery to Charles. That should get him chatting even more than the candy did."

"You are an evil genius, my friend. And I'm glad you're on the side of good and right."

I smiled. "Sometimes."

"Before we go see him, I'd like to know more about the family."

"Yeah, I was thinking that, too." I told him what I'd learned about the rental cars. "Someone could have taken the other car, followed Karen to the woods, then waited for Charles to wander off."

Ray frowned. "And killed her?"

"Well, it might not have started out that way. Suppose one of her brothers wanted to talk to her privately. She's always got Charles hanging around. But they know Charles wanders when he and his mother are hiking. So the brother follows them, hoping to get Karen aside."

"An argument ensues and then escalates," Ray said.

"Especially if it's about a sore subject, like Charles. Say being together at this hotel has shown the family that Charles needs to be sent away to school. Jules, for example, is delegated to talk to Karen."

"She wouldn't agree."

"And then Jules, or Leo, or even Jules's wife, gets frustrated and jabs her." I mimed an open-handed push with my right hand. "Not a killing blow. Could even be a slap."

"Enough so that she loses her balance and goes down."

I pushed back my chair and stood up. "Let's head to Kahala and test this theory out. And then on our way back, we can pick up the coffee and take it to Charles."

"Hold on, cowboy," Ray said, motioning me back to my seat. "Can we think this through? Like who do we suspect? And is there anyone we can reliably remove from consideration?"

I said down. "I doubt that Karen's mother Belle has the means to do this. She's seventy years old and I don't see her climbing a mountain trail after her daughter and pushing her over. She strikes me as the type to get her way by bossiness rather than physical violence."

"I'll take that under advisement. My mother is nearly seventy and she's strong as an ox."

"There are two teenagers along for this visit." I grabbed my iPad and scanned through to my notes. "David and Jessica are both old enough to drive, as long as Jules paid the underage driver fee." I shrugged. "Even if he didn't, one of them could still grab the keys and sneak out."

"Motive?"

"Fed up with cousin Charles? Jessica seems to feel sorry for him, even though she called him a creep, but David didn't appear to be a big fan." I thought for a minute.

I remembered what my sister-in-law Tatiana had said about the tuition at Pepperdine. "I wonder... if Belle is having financial problems, might that impact Jules's ability to pay tuition for his kids at Tulane?" I turned to my computer and did a quick search. "With no financial aid, tuition alone is running him over a hundred grand for both kids."

"And with Karen and Charles out of the way, there might be more money to pay their bills," Ray said. "I can see that. But let's move on. Three adults, right?"

"Jules and his wife Emeline, and Leo. Any one of the three could have been delegated to have 'the talk' with Karen."

"What do we know about them?" Ray asked.

"I didn't get much farther in research beyond education and property ownership."

"Let's see what kind of dirt we can dig up then," Ray said. He wiggled his fingers and smiled.

We agreed he'd take Jules and Emeline, and I'd look into Leo.

As is often the case, research became a rabbit hole I could fall into. Leo Fontenot popped up frequently in gossip columns and local news stories. He was an uptown boy with a taste for downtown girls, and there was some implied snickering when he married a Vietnamese nail technician. After his divorce he dated black women, Asian women, and a few who were dismissively called "yats," which I recalled was a snobby term for the less financially secure.

So even if Leo happened to date a white woman, she was someone who wouldn't fit in with his upper-crust family.

It was harder to figure out what Leo did for a living. His family had been rich plantation owners, so it was possible that he was the beneficiary of a family trust. But I kept digging, and occasionally I found a mention of Leo at a luncheon for real estate executives, or his picture among a group of other men and women in the business.

He didn't have a real estate salesman's license, though. And he wasn't buying, renovating and flipping properties—I would have seen evidence of that in official property records. When I finished, I called Belle Fontenot's suite at the Albergo and made arrangements to come out to update her and her family on the case.

"What time?"

I looked at the clock. "Say eleven? And can you have the whole family there so we can ask some questions?"

"What kind of questions?"

"Routine," I said. "We just need to establish where everyone who knew your daughter was at the time of her death."

"You think one of us killed her?"

"No, not at all," I lied. "It's just routine. Filling out forms, checking boxes."

She snorted. "Fine. I'll have everyone here in the suite at eleven."

Ray looked up from his computer and said he was good to go any time. We compared notes as we drove out to Kahala. Though Jules was a name partner in his firm, it didn't appear to be a very successful one. They had lost one of the name partners, and his division, a year before, and the reorganization had led them to smaller offices with a less prestigious address. "His son David says he has a temper, and had some incidents in the past."

"All dismissed," Ray said. "Though I can see that evidence."

"How about the kids?"

"Both of them at Tulane. Neither of them appears to work, which means someone is paying out their tuition and fees."

"That plantation used to be over a hundred acres, but each generation has been selling land. Think there's any money left?"

"The initial charge for the stay in Kahala must have put a big burden on Belle's credit card to have it denied halfway through the visit. Though it's possible that credit card is tied to a checking account, and there's more money in investments."

We parked in the guest lot and I was disappointed to see that there was no attendant we could ask about the movement of the Fontenots' cars.

As we walked through the parking lot, Ray said, "You've already spoken to these people a couple of times. Why don't I take the adults, and you take the kids."

"Because I did so well with Charles?"

"Because I can ask Belle and her sons and daughter-in-law questions you've already asked, and we can compare answers."

"You know, sometimes I forget what it's like having a partner." I grinned. "Happy times."

He elbowed me, and I stepped back and held up my hands. "Hey, watch where you're pushing."

In a low voice, he began to sing the Culture Club hit, "I'll Tumble 4 Ya."

I was still laughing when we got to the elevator.

Chapter 24
Family Interviews

I knocked on the door, and was surprised that it was answered by Jimmy Ah Wang.

He looked as surprised to see me as I was to see him. "Kimo," he said. "And Ray. I thought you left town."

"Rumors of my departure have reversed," Ray said. "I'm back."

Jimmy was a witness in my first big case as a detective, and being honest with the police had resulted in his father's kicking him out of the house for being gay. Back then he had been a skinny, shy teen with a cockscomb of dyed blond hair. I had arranged for my godmother to take him in, and he'd blossomed, graduating from college and growing into a solid young man who worked in social services for the state.

"What are you doing here?" I asked.

"Representing an orphaned minor on behalf of the state." He nodded his head backward.

"But he's not an orphan," I said. "His father is here in Honolulu. Didn't the Fontenots tell you that?"

He looked surprised. "No, they said they were the boy's only family. You have the father's name?"

"I'll text you," I said.

"OK, well, I'm done here. I'll talk to you later."

He walked out, and I went into the suite first, and introduced Ray. Time had not improved their personalities; they all looked like rejected cast members of a rich-people reality show. The men wore Rolex watches, Emeline a chunky necklace of gold and emeralds. The perfect fit of their polo shirts and slacks, and Emeline's shift dress, said money.

Then I shook hands with David and Jessica. They both looked like well-fed, well-tanned specimens of wealthy America, from his Brooks Brothers polo (a logo I'd seen often enough in high school at Punahou) and her white crop-top with the Fendi logo across the bottom.

I picked David first, because he was the oldest, and he'd expect that. "Can you step out onto the balcony with me for a couple of minutes? I just have a couple of questions."

"Remember that you come from a family of lawyers," his father said.

"Like I could ever forget it." His voice was almost a snarl.

I opened the door to the balcony, while behind me I heard Ray explain that he'd be taking the rest of the family into one of the bedrooms one at a time.

"I'm sorry for your loss," I said, when David and I were out on the balcony with the door closed behind us. The Pacific was straight ahead, a white sandy beach shaded by palm trees and with a serried row of wooden chairs with blue and white striped awnings.

David shrugged.

"Were you and your cousin close?"

"Are you kidding? Have you heard about him? He's a freak. Either he's babbling about his leaf collection or he's exploding over the way the waitress didn't bring all his side dishes on separate plates."

"Must have been difficult."

"We usually stay away from him and Aunt Karen. Only like once or twice year, for Grand'Mere's birthday or Christmas."

Unruly Son

"Your parents see him more often?"

David shook his head. "My dad and Aunt Karen didn't get along. Both lawyers, right? Each of them always arguing their points. In addition to my dad's temper, which I told you about. No way I'm going to law school."

"Anything specific they argued about?"

He narrowed his eyes at me. "You're not trying to pin this on my father, are you? Because he's one of the most prominent lawyers in New Orleans. He'll eat a coconut cowboy like you alive."

That was an interesting insult, a coconut cowboy. Often the term coconut was used to refer to someone who was brown on the outside and white on the inside. Though I had a pretty good tan, and my Hawaiian ancestors had darker skin, I usually passed for white, except for the epicanthic fold over my eyelids.

"I'm not trying to pin anything on anyone," I said mildly. "Just trying to get an idea of the family dynamic."

"There were usually two things they argued about. Money, and Charles. We all believed that Charles should be sent away somewhere. Dad thought Aunt Karen was wasting her life and her brains dealing with Charles twenty-four-seven. And that she should stop draining the family money by not working."

He looked at his watch. "Listen, is this going to take long? Because Jess and I have a tennis court reserved at eleven-thirty."

"Just a couple more questions and then I'll let you go. When was the last time you saw your Aunt Karen?"

He frowned. "Must have been last Sunday night at dinner. Charles had another one of his outbursts and Karen took him away."

"You didn't see her Monday morning?"

He shook his head. "Nah, I slept in. Vacation, right? Jess and I were out at the hotel club until late Sunday."

"What time would you say you woke up?"

"About ten-thirty. Jess and I had a tennis court reserved for eleven, and we got there just in time to claim it."

I thanked him and he walked inside. He said, "You're next," to his sister, and she joined me on the balcony.

"I think it's just terrible that you all left Charles deserted on that mountain for days," she began, before I could even provide my condolences. "I mean, that's ridiculous. When exactly did Aunt Karen die?"

"The Medical Examiner puts the time of death at late last Monday morning," I said. I started to ask where she was then, but she cut me off.

"That's Monday, Tuesday, Wednesday and Thursday," she said, counting on her fingers. "Three and a half days. He's almost feral anyway, but to leave him out there with no food and water." She jabbed me in the chest. "That's criminal."

"I agree," I said mildly. "And if your family had provided the correct license plate information to us at the start, we might have been able to find him much sooner."

"What do you mean?"

"Your family had two rental cars at the time, right? One in your father's name and one in your aunt's. When your family reported her missing, they gave us the wrong information about the rental car. It wasn't until the next day that we learned we had wasted a whole day looking for a car that was still here in the parking lot."

"Oh. Yeah. I remember my dad and Uncle Leo arguing about that." She shook her head. "I know David told you about our dad's temper, but Uncle Leo is even worse, because he doesn't have the brains to back up his arguments, and he goes nutso. He actually punched my dad in the chest last year, and my dad would have called the cops on him if Grand'Mere hadn't intervened."

Interesting. So bad tempers ran in the family, at least on the male side.

"So. When was the last time you saw your aunt and your cousin?"

She repeated the same story her brother had told, about a disruption at Sunday dinner, and then going out with David to the hotel club. The two of them were sharing a two-bedroom suite with their parents, and she confirmed they had played tennis on Monday morning together, at around the time Karen was killed.

"How would you characterize this vacation?" I asked. "I mean, before your aunt and Charles disappeared."

"Miserable. Grand'Mere controls all the money, you know. My dad pretends to be this rich lawyer, but we all live on an allowance from her. This whole vacation we've had to bow and scrape to her highness. I can't wait to get out of here."

That was interesting. If her grandmother controlled all the money, why had her credit card exceeded the limit? A simple error, or something more?

"One last question, something I'm curious about. What does your Uncle Leo do for a living?"

She laughed. "He's a waste of space. All he wants to do is drink and screw and take drugs." She frowned. "Or at least that's what my parents say. I don't have any experience with any of that myself."

"Good for you." I thanked her and let her go back inside, and she and her brother left for their tennis date.

Ray was in the bedroom with Leo, and Jules came up to me as I walked inside. "I hope you weren't badgering my children. They had almost nothing to do with their aunt and cousin."

"I got that impression. If you don't mind my asking, what kind of law do you practice? Criminal?"

It looked like he'd smelled something awful. "Not at all. Trusts and estates, primarily."

"So you'd be the right person to ask if your sister had a will."

He glared at me. "Of course."

"And I think as an attorney, you'll recognize the concept of cui bono, and that you won't be offended if I ask the general terms of that will."

"My sister was virtually penniless," he said. "She gave up an excellent law career and spent everything she had saved on supporting herself and taking care of Charles."

Interesting. "As Charles is a minor child, I assume she made provisions for him in her will."

"She did." I could see he was resisting giving this information—something he thought ought to be private, but as an attorney he knew the contents of a will would eventually be public, and he might as well tell me.

"In the event that she was unable to take care of Charles, she named me as his guardian. She recognized that there was no way that Emeline or I could provide him the care he needs, so she directed me to enroll him in a residential facility for young people with Oppositional Defiant Disorder, in a suburb of Chicago."

"And will you be sending Charles there, when you're ready to leave Honolulu?"

He glanced over at his mother, who remained tight-lipped. "There is some question of the ability to pay the fees required at this school," he finally said. "Until we get that resolved we can't make a decision."

Ray came out of the bedroom then with Leo, and we thanked the family for their cooperation. "I have asked this question several times and I have yet to receive a satisfactory answer," Belle Fontenot said. "When will I be able to have my daughter's remains released to us for cremation?"

I looked at Ray. "The Medical Examiner has assured us he'll be able to issue a death certificate by the end of the week," I said.

I knew I was locking us in, but Doc Takayama had already told me that was as long as he could reasonably delay.

"I will make arrangements, then," Belle said. "You can see yourselves out."

Chapter 25
Farewell to Thee

"A lot of information to digest," I said, as Ray and I rode down in the elevator. "What do you say we treat ourselves to what is undeniably expensive coffee here at the hotel and compare notes?"

"We're going to a coffee shop from here to get that stuff for Charles, aren't we? How far is it?"

I put Big Mo's into my phone. "Only a mile," I said. "Turns out they have several branches."

"Then why don't we stop there?"

I agreed, though I had been looking forward to a luxurious Italian café experience. "Before we leave the hotel, I wanted to check the alibi Jessica and David gave me for Monday. They said they had a tennis court reserved that morning at eleven, and they played."

We walked through the hotel's overblown lobby, Italian marble everywhere, to the tennis courts, where we found the man in charge, a lean, well-tanned Hawaiian in white shorts and a white tennis shirt with the Albergo logo. His name badge read Ori.

I showed him my badge and asked if he could check his records for the previous Monday.

"We're supposed to ask for a search warrant in cases like this," he said.

"We're just confirming the Fontenots were where they said they'd be," I said.

"In that case, I can confirm they weren't without even looking."

Ray and I shared a glance. "Can you tell me why?" I asked.

Ori sighed. "I don't want to make a big deal out of this, all right? The hotel doesn't like bad publicity."

"If we don't need the information for a court case it won't go any farther."

"I've had my eye on one of the staff for a while, a boy named Wilbert. He smelled like pakalolo sometimes." He held up his hand. "Not that I have a problem with what anybody does in his spare time, but the hotel has a very strict anti-drug policy. Last Monday, I happened to look through some security cam footage and I spotted Wilbert talking to the Fontenot boy, heads down, the girl in the background looking around for anyone who might see them."

I saw where this was gong.

"I spoke to Wilbert that afternoon and he admitted selling them an ounce of pakalolo. I fired him on the spot. But I didn't report the incident to hotel management or the police because ... well, you understand."

"Thank you, Ori," I said. "This has been very helpful. If we need to go further, we'll come back and get Wilbert's information. But otherwise we'll keep quiet."

We didn't say anything more until we were off the hotel grounds. "Does this destroy David and Jessica's alibi, or just change it?" I asked, as we climbed into the SUV.

"We'd have to get hold of the security camera footage and check the time," Ray said. "But in my experience, when somebody gets hold of an ounce of marijuana, it's not to fortify themselves for murder. Instead they find some remote corner where they can smoke, get high, and go into a happy place."

"What about the rest of the family? What did you think?"

"I want to organize it in my head first," he said. "Give me a few minutes."

So we were silent for the drive past the back of Diamond Head to the coffee shop, across the street from the Honolulu Zoo.

I was pleased to see that they could prepare a big container of Café du Monde coffee for us to go and ordered that as well as a café mocha with coconut milk and chocolate syrup for myself. In keeping with their location across from the zoo, it was called a coco-monkey.

Ray kept it simple with a very large American coffee, and we sat down at a table under a palm tree outside with our devices, and started typing up what we had learned at the hotel.

"I almost forgot. I have to send Jimmy Ah Wang Omari's information."

I typed a quick email to Jimmy and attached a link to the family tree, along with Omari's phone number.

A server in a khaki shirt with a palm-leaf badge brought our coffees as we worked. I was halfway through mine by the time I finished writing up my interviews with David and Jessica Fontenot as well as what I had learned from their father, and what we'd heard from Ori the tennis pro.

"I wish there was a way we could figure how much money Belle Fontenot has," I said. "It's possible that she's land-rich and cash-poor."

"She's been supporting all three of her kids and maintaining that estate," Ray said. "She told me that she set up college savings plans for David and Jessica when they were born, but the income hasn't kept up with the rising cost of Tulane tuition, room and board, so she's paying out of pocket for them, too."

I nodded. "Jessica said her family is practically penniless, and they have to rely on her grandmother for everything."

"Do you think she doesn't have the money to pay for Charles's tuition at this facility in Chicago?" Ray asked. "Is that why Jules is being cagey?"

"And why they're leaving him in the hospital? I'd say that's a good possibility."

Ray frowned. "So how did Karen's death benefit anyone?"

I sipped my coffee and went over everything I knew about the family. "There's something interesting about Leo," I said finally. "He seems to hang out with real estate folks a lot. But he lives in a rental apartment and doesn't have a salesman's license."

"Could he be shopping around his mother's property without her permission, hoping to put together a deal she can't refuse?"

A band struck up at the Zoo across the street, and I recognized the tune as Aloha 'Oe, the song written by Queen Lili'uokalani, which meant "Farewell to Thee."

As we watched, several school buses pulled up and loaded up with kids. They played the song again and again until the last of the buses was gone.

I flexed my fingers over the keyboard and started typing. "Belle Fontenot is listed at an address on Patterson Road in New Orleans. The area is called Algiers Point, directly across the Mississippi River from the French Quarter. Karen Fontenot is listed at the same address."

"Personal residence or business address or both?" Ray asked.

I typed some more. "She has a law license, registered at the home on Patterson Road, but it's inactive. She also had a license as an arbitrator and it looks like she did some work in dispute resolution, but only part time."

Ray said, "According to the property records for Orleans Parish, that address has been in the Fontenot family since before property sales were recorded, because the only dollar figure associated with the property is the value of the land, which is listed at ten million dollars for tax purposes."

"A nice round number," I said.

"But a friend of Julie's comes from an old Philadelphia family, and she always said they were real estate rich and cash poor. Most of their money was tied up in the family mansion, which no one could agree on selling."

"The Fontenots may be in the same situation," I said. A little more digging brought up an interesting article from the *Times-Picayune* from several years before. Terre Riche Plantation was situated on a bluff overlooking the Mississippi River across from downtown New Orleans. It had once spanned a hundred acres, but now all that remained was the mansion house and ten acres of land.

There were rumors in the press that developers had their eyes on the property. Because of its elevation, it was relatively safe from flood waters, and there was speculation that several condo towers could be erected there with magnificent views of the river and the city skyline.

"What if Jules and Leo want to sell the plantation, and Karen was resisting, because she didn't want to move Charles?"

I beeped the SUV, and we got in. "I think Belle is the one who makes the decisions, but I wouldn't be surprised if she has a soft spot for Karen."

"With Karen out of the way, Leo and Jules can pressure their mother. And they get Charles shipped away as a bonus."

"How do people think like this?" I asked. "Oh, we can kill our sister and get our nephew sent away, and then everything will be rosy?"

"Because they're human," Ray said. "You're letting your feelings for Charles Fontenot get in the way of this investigation. I agree, he's been hit with a sucky blow. Lost his mom, most likely going to lose his home and his leaf collection and get sent away. But in the end, he's collateral damage. We have to focus on Karen Fontenot's murder."

"This whole case makes me sick. Every time we turn around, Charles Fontenot is in the middle. And we don't know if he's a killer."

"Then we ought to go speak to him," Ray said.

Chapter 26
Coffee and Cocktails

Ray called and established that Charles Fontenot was still at the Queen's Medical Center, and I ordered the kid the largest size of the chicory coffee he liked. We drove over there, and just to be further on his good side, I stopped at the gift shop, where I remembered the kind of candy bars he'd liked and picked up a few more.

Jeremy Hoult was on duty in front of Charles's room. We didn't really need a cop there anymore, but no one had bothered to tell that to dispatch, and I figured it was good for us to have another set of eyes around.

"You going to the QOLE meeting this evening?" Jeremy asked me.

"I think so. How about you?"

"I'm psyched. Sometimes I feel like the only gay cop in town. I mean, after you. But it's different being a detective and being on patrol. I hope there will be other guys there I can talk to."

Charles was playing the same game when we walked in. "Candy man!" he crowed. "What did you bring me?"

I was glad that he remembered the candy, and not the meltdown. "You like Café du Monde coffee?" I asked, showing him the big cup.

"You can't get that here."

"Sure you can." I handed him the cup. "Try it. Tell me if it's just like it is back home."

He cautiously opened the lid and took a sip, and his eyes lit up. "It's awesome!"

My heart warmed that I'd been able to bring a small bit of happiness to this kid whose life was falling apart.

I introduced Ray, but Charles was too busy with his coffee to pay attention. "Had any good visitors since I was here?"

He shook his head. "My father came for a while. I never met him before."

"Oh," I said. "Did you get along?"

He shrugged. "We've been email buddies. That's what he called it. He said he was glad to meet me in person."

"And you? Were you glad to see him?"

"He didn't bring candy."

I took the hint and pulled a bar out of the bag. "Like this?"

"You are the dude of dudes," he said. Then he looked confused. "That's what Uncle Leo used to say to me. Is that a good thing?"

"It's a very good thing." Since Charles and I were cooking with gas, I pulled up a chair close to him and took the lead.

We talked for a while about his leaf collection, and how a nurse and the police officer had taken him outside the day before so he could collect some more. "They won't let me have an iron, though."

"That sucks." Charles and I talked for a couple of minutes, and then we were interrupted by an imperious voice behind us.

"What are you doing here?"

I looked behind me and saw Belle Charles, accompanied by her granddaughter Jessica. Charles assumed she was talking to him. "They won't let me leave, Grand'Mere."

"I was speaking to the policeman," Belle said.

"I came to bring your grandson some coffee," I said. "Chicory, the way he likes it."

"Well, you can leave now. We have family business to discuss."

"I want the candy man to stay!" Charles said. "You can go."

"I brought you a candy bar too," Jessica said. "Snickers. Your favorite."

I stood up. "We'll come back another time, Charles. Bring you more candy."

"He doesn't need any more candy," Belle said. "He eats too much already. He'll get fat along with all his other problems."

I ignored her, and followed Ray out the door. Jessica looked at us both and sighed as she shut the door behind us.

"What do you think Belle is doing here?" I asked, as Ray and I walked down the hospital corridor. "Come to check him out?"

"I doubt it. Maybe they've come to tell him about that school in Chicago."

"Interesting that Belle came with Jessica, not either of her sons. But Jessica seemed to be the most caring about Charles."

By then it was late afternoon. We stopped at the Kope Bean across from the hospital and I checked my email. The techs had been able to get into Karen's phone, and they'd have the results for us the next morning. I also spotted the reminder that QOLE was having its initial meeting that evening.

I called Mike. "You want to go to this QOLE meeting with me?"

"Got it on my calendar. Dinner afterwards? I'll get my father to feed and walk Roby."

"Works for me."

When I hung up I realized that this might be a good opportunity for Sergei to network with people from other agencies, see if there might be somewhere he could fit in. I called him. "Hey, brah, you busy?"

"Why? You want a blow job?"

"Sergei. You know that's not going to happen, so why do you bother?"

"You never know."

I was already regretting my decision to call him, but I plunged forward. "A woman I work with is starting a new organization for

Queer Oahu Law Enforcement folks. First meeting this evening downtown. I thought you might want to check it out, see if you get information from anyone about jobs."

"That's great, Kimo. I really appreciate it."

I gave him the time and place. "But this is not a gay bar. It's a professional group. Try to keep your dick in your pants, all right?"

"Do my best."

We worked out that Ray would take my SUV back to Aiea Heights, leave it at my house and walk the rest of the way up the hill. I'd ride home after the meeting with Mike.

Queen had directed us to meet at The Koa Tree, a relatively new bar a few blocks from the Alapai Headquarters. It been built around a giant koa tree that had lived on the spot for decades, reaching a height of nearly fifty feet. The ceilings were high and the furnishings had an island vibe, with wooden tables and thatched roofing. I met Mike on the sidewalk outside about an hour later, still worrying about my decision to invite Sergei.

"You're sure you're up for this?" I asked.

He frowned. "I'm not the scared guy I was twelve years ago when I met you," he said. "I've matured, and the world has changed around us. Yeah, I still think who I sleep with is my personal business, but if I have to sacrifice a little of my privacy to help some kid avoid the angst of coming out, or even suicide, it's worth it."

"And that's why I love you," I said, leaning up to give him a quick peck on the cheek.

Just before we walked inside, I said, "I told Sergei about this. I hope it doesn't come back to bite me in the ass."

"You invited a wild card like Sergei? What were you thinking?"

"He said he was looking for a job. Maybe there will be someone here he can talk to."

"Or maybe he'll strip down to a jock strap and dance on a table," Mike said. "This might be interesting after all."

We were directed to a small private room off to one side. Queen was there in her HPD uniform, talking with Jeremy Hoult. There

Unruly Son

were a few other people in the room already too, most of them strangers to me. I was surprised at the turnout, but Queen Jones was a marvel of persuasion and determination.

Sergei came in a few minutes later, but he didn't need me to introduce him—he walked right up to one of the park rangers, a slim young woman, and started talking to her.

Queen called the meeting to order once everyone had drinks, either caffeinated or alcoholic. "I'd like us all to agree that this is a safe space," she said. "We can't fix problems unless we're honest in facing them, and we can't be honest if we're worried someone will be carrying tales on us."

There was general agreement. We all introduced ourselves and our agencies. It was a sign of progress in the Aloha State that we had representatives of almost every law enforcement group in the islands, from an FBI agent to a couple of park rangers.

Then each of us talked about the atmosphere in our teams. In general, the younger people were more optimistic and felt more comfortable, while the older folks talked more about the obstacles they'd overcome.

"I had a homophobic boss when I came out," I said, when it was my turn. "I think I was probably the first high-profile LEO to come out and he didn't like it. I was suspended and had to go in for administrative review."

My voice shook as I remembered the trauma of that time. "I don't know if any of you will remember, but I was on the TV news and in the papers."

"I remember," Queen said. "It was a real watershed moment."

"I was only fourteen," Jeremy said. "I knew that I liked guys, and that I wanted to be a cop, but I didn't see how those two things could come together until you came out."

"Thank you both," I said. "It means a lot to me to know that I might have inspired someone. I could only do it because of two people. The first of those is Officer Kitty Cardozo."

The audience swiveled its attention to Kitty. She'd changed out of her uniform and into slacks and a polo shirt. "Kitty came out to her stepdad, Lieutenant Jim Sampson from District 1, and that started him on his path to understanding. When I was at my lowest point, he offered me a job and a safe place to work."

"To be fair, Jim has always been a great guy," Kitty said. "My mom is a flake, but Jim was there for me and often told me that he loved me no matter what happened. So it wasn't hard to come out to him. He looked around HPD and saw the prejudice, and he started walking the path that allowed him to open up to Kimo."

"I'm another guy who's been inspired by Kimo," Sergei said, and immediately I tensed. What was he going to say? That I'd given him a great blow job once upon a time, when Mike and I were not together?

"I've been kind of a screw-up," Sergei said. "Part of that was my avoidance of my sexuality. I grew up in Alaska and I was a wild kid, because I could see that I didn't fit in with my family or my culture. But then my sister married Kimo's brother, and I saw the way his ohana circled around him. It's because of his example that I'm trying to get my life in order, and I think I'd like to try law enforcement. I'm a late bloomer, though, so I'd appreciate any advice on an agency that would take me on."

"Do you think he's bullshitting us?" I whispered to Mike.

He looked at me, and there was something very deep in his eyes. "Sometimes you don't recognize the effect you have on people."

I thought about that as the conversation ebbed and flowed around me. Finally Queen proposed QOLE as a name for our group, and promised to send some guidelines on how we could organize around to us all.

I tuned out the basics of establishing a mission statement and how we hoped to interface with the department to make sure queer recruits knew they were welcome across the various agencies on the island. I was surprised when Mike spoke up.

"I checked the websites of every agency, and each one has the county's diversity statement linked to their home page," he said. "I've

Unruly Son

been reviewing the policies and procedures at HFD and making notes of places where our language can be more inclusive."

I hadn't known he was doing that—but then, for the last two weeks I'd been busy with Ray's return and Karen Fontenot's disappearance.

A woman from the Coast Guard, who I recognized from my stint at the FBI, said she was working on the same issues with her agency. Jeremy Hoult asked if our intranet list of approved physicians and pharmacies that accepted our insurance could be altered to indicate those who were responsive to LGBTQ+ issues.

"That's a great idea," Queen said, and she typed it into her iPad.

We went through a number of other issues, like frequency of meetings and adding preferred pronouns to our email signatures.

"I think that's really important," a Filipina woman said. "My first name is so unusual people don't know how to address me in emails."

We talked about that for a while, what kind of gender-neutral salutations we could use, and by then my coffee cup was dry and my stomach was grumbling.

Queen asked for volunteers for subcommittees, and we set up another mass meeting for a month later. As we were preparing to leave, a young man I didn't recognize came up to us. "Captain Riccardi, I'm a probie in the Makiki Station, and I wanted to tell you how much I appreciate your being here, and your being out in the department. I probably would never have begun the academy if I hadn't heard about you."

Mike shook his hand. "What's your name?"

"Evan Portuondo."

"Any relation to Lidia?" I asked.

He turned to me. "She's my cousin."

"And a great officer," I said. "If you're anything like her I'm sure you'll be a credit to your department."

"Keep in touch, Evan," Mike said. "I'll be over in Makiki in a couple of weeks to teach a course. See you then."

Evan left, and Sergei joined us. "Thanks for inviting me, Kimo," he said. "I talked to both of the rangers and got all the info I need to apply. They said there's a shortage of people qualified in native studies, so if I study up I could even get a position as a docent. I think I'd really like that, talking to people about the history of the place, giving them maps and so on."

He leaned in close to me. "And you'll be pleased to know that I kept my hands to myself, though that Jeremy Hoult was pretty tasty."

I didn't know what to say, so I just shook my head. He walked out, and I noticed that Jeremy was one of the last people left in the room. He headed toward us, and I said to Mike, "If he says he finds Sergei tasty I am NOT playing matchmaker."

Instead of Sergei or QOLE, though, he wanted to talk about Charles Fontenot. "He was pretty agitated after his grandmother and his cousin left this afternoon," he said. "He started yelling that he didn't want to go back to New Orleans. That his mother had promised him if anything happened to her he would go to a school with other kids like him."

I turned to Mike. "Apparently there's a school in Chicago that his mother had picked out. But some question of where the money to pay for it will come from."

"The nurses had to come in and restrain him again," Jeremy said. "Just thought you ought to know."

I thanked him. "It's a tough situation and I don't see how it's going to be resolved in anybody's favor," I said. "But I'm going to try."

Chapter 27
Complex Net

Mike had driven over to the Koa Tree from the fire department garage, and we walked to where he'd parked. "How do you feel?" he asked me.

"Weird. This evening reminded me how public my life was for a while. That it seemed like everyone on the island knew I was the gay cop. And how uncomfortable that made me."

"I understand that. I saw you in the news too."

"And did I inspire you?"

"No, you scared the shit out of me. Because I thought that could be me, in the news like that." He looked over at me. "And because I was crushing on you and I knew it would be impossible for us to be together, if everyone knew about you."

"And here we are, twelve years later," I said. "We surfed those incoming waves and we survived to surf another day."

"I use a different metaphor. I fought my way through that fire. And I came out stronger."

It felt so good to be with him, after all those years together, heading back to the restaurant where we'd first begun falling in love.

That good feeling carried over when we got home, and we had to shut Roby out of the bedroom for a while, which did not make him happy. But after we were done, we both showered him with affection, so he got over it.

Ray and Julie had bought a car by then, but she was using it to drive back and forth to the University of Hawai'i campus. So just as we'd started when Ray joined HPD, I was his chauffeur once again. At least it gave us extra time to talk about the case, and the next morning I brought up what I'd heard at the QOLE meeting.

"Something Sergei said reminded me of something," I said.

"Something good or something bad?"

"Something about the case. He said something about maps. When I went into the park where I found Karen Fontenot, the first thing I did was pick up a map. But we didn't find a map with Karen's effects."

"Couldn't Charles have run off with it?"

"Possibility. But part of our theory is that Karen was looking at the map, and not at where she was going, which is how she fell."

"In which case we should have found a map nearby. We'll have to ask Charles when we talk to him again."

"Oh, something else I learned last night," I said, and I repeated what Jeremy Hoult had said.

"So Charles wants to go to Chicago," Ray said. "Do you think money is the hang-up?"

"Could be. We'll see what happens when Doc Takayama releases Karen's body."

When we finally got to the Alapai Headquarters, we were able to see what the techs had dug up on Karen's phone. "Lots of calls to the 504 area code," Ray said. "Which makes sense. Calling back to New Orleans for various reasons."

"Look at this, though," I said, pointing. "She called these two numbers what, five or six times each? And the last call was the morning she fell."

We did a quick reverse search. The two common numbers belonged to her brothers. The last one to speak with her had been

Leo, around the time we thought she and Charles had arrived at the park.

"All three of them are in Honolulu," I said. "In the same hotel. Why are they talking on the phone, instead of in person?"

"She always had Charles around her somewhere," Ray said. "Maybe she was talking to her brothers about him, and didn't want him to know."

"About what, though? You think she wanted to send him to that school in Chicago, and she was trying to borrow money from them?"

"I don't know," Ray said. "She doesn't seem like the kind of mom who'd want to send her son away, and I got the sense from her will that the school was only a choice if she couldn't take care of him."

"Jeremy Hoult said when Belle was visiting yesterday, she and Charles argued about the school. I'd like to find out what Charles wants to do."

"And we should talk to Omari Fontenot again, too. Is he going to be Charles's legal guardian? Does Charles inherit some money?"

"According to Jules Fontenot, Karen was broke. But there may be a trust for Charles that no one has mentioned yet. He did say that his mother had established education trusts for both David and Jessica, though they weren't covering the cost of Tulane and he was paying out of pocket."

I called Omari and found that he was still at the hostel in Manoa, though he was hoping to transfer to a campground for the weekend. I let him know that we'd be over in a half hour.

We found him in the same place, at an outside table, sitting in the shade of a tall, spreading kiawe tree, which was nicknamed the tree of life in South America, where it originated. Its pods could be used as livestock fodder, turned into molasses, brewed into a tea or even used to make beer. Though none of that seemed to matter to Omari Fontenot, who looked pretty depressed.

"Not what I expected from this trip," he said. "My fault, in part. I should have realized that the public campgrounds close on Wednesday and Thursday. I guess I had this idea that Karen's family, being rich and all, would invite me to join them at the hotel once they met me."

He looked at us. "And of course I couldn't anticipate Karen's death or anything that happened from it. Have you found out anything else yet?"

"We're still exploring leads," I said. "What's your plan with regard to Charles? You could apply for custody. If you're sure a DNA test would prove your relationship."

"I've seen the boy," Omari said. "He's mine, all right. I don't need a DNA test to tell me. But I also know there's no way I could give him the care he needs. I barely scrape by on my own." He held up his hand and started ticking off his fingers. "I drive an Uber, and I also deliver groceries for Uber Eats. I work ten hours a week stocking shelves at an organic grocery, and I pick up seasonal jobs when I can, like raking leaves and shoveling snow."

He looked up at us. "And I already have a boy I look after. Not mine biologically, but I volunteer with Big Brothers and they assigned DeMarcus to me. We play basketball together, and I take him to games and to movies when I can afford it."

"The family wants to send Charles to a school in Chicago," I said. "How do you feel about that?"

"Whatever's best for Charles. Of course I wish the school was closer to San Francisco, but now that I know he exists I'll try and see him sometimes. And we can email, like we have been doing."

I looked at Ray. We both knew the last question we had to ask. "This is just a formality, you understand," he said. "But we have to ask you if you have an alibi for last Monday morning, when Karen was killed."

"I have my receipt from the campground," he said. He pulled his wallet out of his pocket and showed it to us. All it said, though, was that he had checked in there around nine PM on Sunday, the day before she died.

Then he said, "Oh, wait. I bought some snacks from a surf rental shop near the beach on Monday morning. Let me see if I have the

Unruly Son

receipt for that." He rummaged in his wallet for a minute and then pulled out a wrinkled piece of paper. Indeed, he had been at North Shore Surf Rentals on Monday morning at 10:17 AM, where he had purchased a soda and a bag of chips.

I pulled out my iPad and took a picture of the receipt, then thanked him and returned it.

"Will you make sure that Charles knows how to get a hold of me?" he asked. "I don't know if they take his phone away or anything at that school."

"I'll make sure," I said.

We walked back to where we'd parked and I made a couple of notes about the conversation. "So if Omari Fontenot is definitely out as a suspect, where does that leave us?" I asked Ray.

"We still have the possibility of a stranger, but that seems pretty remote at this point," Ray said. "Which brings us back to the family. Uncle Jules, Aunt Emeline, Uncle Leo and the two cousins."

"Then I guess it's back to Charles," I said.

Though it was well out of our way, we swung past Big Mo's to get Charles another chicory coffee, as well as caffeine for ourselves, and then a drugstore with a better selection of candy than the hospital gift shop.

There was no officer in front of Charles's room, and the nurse on duty told us that the last officer there had told her there was no need to guard Charles anymore. "Where do they get these ideas?" I grumbled. "You'd think someone could have told us."

Charles was playing his video game again, but once more was delighted to see me, and to get a coffee. We chatted for a couple of minutes, and then I said, "I hate to bring up bad memories, but I have to. Do you remember the last time you saw your mom?"

He nodded, between sipping his coffee and breaking bits off his candy bar. "She was looking at the map. She's really into maps. She always has to have a map wherever we go. I don't care. I like to explore."

"She was looking at the map, and you walked away?"

He nodded. "But it was okay, because Uncle Dude came up to talk to her."

I looked at Ray. "Uncle Dude?"

"Uncle Leo. You know he called me the dude of dudes. That's a good thing, right?"

"It is. I'm surprised. I thought your Uncle Leo stayed back at the hotel."

"We thought so, too. Mom was not happy to see him. He took the map from her and stuck it in his pocket. He said they had to talk. Mom was not happy."

He crossed his arms over his chest in what I figured was an imitation of his mother. "She said, 'Leo, this is my time with Charles.'" He smiled at me. "My time with my mom. We liked to hike. And look for leaves."

I didn't see how people who worked with kids could manage it. I could handle dead bodies with no problem, but every encounter I had with Charles Fontenot broke my heart, as a human being and as a father.

"Did you hear what else they talked about?"

"It was boring. More stuff about selling the house."

"Terre Riche?"

"Rich land. It comes from the French. Our family was French, a long time ago. Now we're New Orleans."

"Your uncle Leo wanted to sell your house?"

He frowned. "My mother didn't want to. Where would she live with me? Where would Grand'Mere live? I didn't want to move."

He started to get agitated, and Ray stepped in. "Yeah, I get that, buddy. Moving sucks."

He looked at Ray as if for the first time. "You don't look Hawaiian. Did you move here from somewhere else?"

"I did. From Philadelphia."

"I went there once with my mom. They had different trees and leaves. We ironed a lot of leaves and saved them. If we moved where would I put my collection?"

From there, nothing that Ray or I could do could stop Charles. I gave him the last couple candy bars and we left before he went into a full meltdown.

"Uncle Dude," Ray said, as we waited for the elevator. "Leo Fontenot told me that he was swimming in the ocean at the time Karen was killed. Alone."

"So essentially no alibi. He could have taken the other rental car and followed Karen and Charles to the park."

"To talk about selling the house," Ray said. "Why go to so much trouble?"

"From what I understand, it was hard to get Karen away from Charles to have a conversation like that. And we know that both Leo and Jules had a number of phone conversations with Karen in the days before she died."

The elevator came and we rode down to the ground floor. The lobby was filled with people coming and going and we didn't talk again until we got to my SUV in the parking garage.

I thought about what we had learned as we drove the few blocks back to the Alapai Headquarters. "That explains why Karen didn't have a map with her when I found her. Leo took it away from her."

Ray nodded, but he looked thoughtful. I waited until we got to headquarters to ask, "What if it wasn't murder? Suppose Leo and Karen were arguing, and she slipped and fell?"

"Then why didn't Leo speak up right away? Call 911 from the park. Hey, my sister fell down a ravine. Send help ASAP."

"I didn't have cell service inside the park," I said. "I had to wait until I got out to call Queen and let her know that I'd found Karen's body."

"But still," Ray said. "If he's a good guy, then he tries to get down to where his sister is. Which we know he couldn't. But then he walked away and left Charles on his own in the woods. Didn't call when he got out of the park. Just went back to the hotel and pretended nothing had happened."

We walked back to our desks in silence, and then grudgingly I admitted, "Because he had to be sure that Karen was dead."

"Exactly."

"So how do we prove this now? All we have is the word of a disturbed young man."

"Somehow the key to this case is in the two rental cars. Somebody had to have seen Leo leave the hotel following Karen."

Sampson was in his office, so Ray and I went over and I knocked on the jamb of his open door. He looked up and said, "I hope you have good news for me."

"I would say we're on the road to good news," I said. "A lot closer than we were yesterday."

We sat in the chairs across from him and explained what we'd done that day. "Hold on. You brought an excitable young man a big cup of coffee?"

I shrank my shoulders down. "It was decaf."

He shook his head. "At least you didn't talk to him, right?"

"Well, here's the thing," I said. "He called me the Candy Man. He was glad to see me. So since I already had a rapport with him…"

"A rapport which ended with him being restrained to the bed."

"This time was different," I protested. "I had Ray there to help me calm him down." Though I paused. "I think he might have had a meltdown after we left, though."

He turned his glare to Ray. "And what did you do while all this was happening? If I recall correctly your charge when you were here previously was to keep your partner from getting into trouble. Did I fail to mention that when I rehired you?"

"In Kimo's defense, he's gotten a lot better over the years," Ray said.

"Which years? The ones you were in Philadelphia?"

"Excuse me," I said, waving my hand. "I'm right here."

The glare turned back to me. "I'm well aware of that."

"What we've been trying to tell you is that we have a suspect and a motive," Ray said. "Thanks to Kimo's conversations with Charles and his cousin Jessica."

Sampson's shoulders relaxed and he leaned back in his chair. "Tell me."

We alternated our explanations. We had only Jessica's word, and the second-hand knowledge that Belle's credit card had been overcharged, that the family was broke, but neither Leo nor Karen worked, and Jules's law firm had scaled back. We had evidence that Terre Riche was worth millions, perhaps even hundreds of millions to the right developer.

And we had Charles telling us that his mother and Uncle Leo had been arguing about selling the house, and she was resisting.

"Though I hate to reverse an opinion so quickly, I will. This is good work. Now how are you going to prove it?"

I looked at Ray, and he shrugged. "We're going to have to interview the family again, based on this new evidence."

"All that's going to do is clarify motive. You need proof. And I can almost guarantee you Charles's testimony will not hold up in court. Jules Fontenot is not only a lawyer, he's the boy's uncle, and he'll parade specialist after specialist who say his memory can't be trusted. That is, if he doesn't have a breakdown on the stand."

"There are ways to accommodate someone with Autism Spectrum Disorder on the witness stand," Ray said. "And ways to combat pre-existing biases by judge and jurors."

Sampson swiveled his chair to face Ray.

He didn't say anything, but Ray looked down at his lap. "One of the courses I took back in Philadelphia covered that."

"I'm sure it did, and I'm sure there are things a prosecuting attorney can consider. For now, I need more concrete evidence before I can even bring this to a prosecutor."

"Understood," I said.

"Then you can go."

We stood up and walked back to our desks. "I had forgotten what it was like to be in the glare of his headlights," Ray said. "Thanks for bringing back the memory." He paused. "And I'm not even the one who got the chocolate or the coffee."

"I bought your coffee at Big Mo's," I protested. "You owe me one."

"Brah, our relationship is a complex net of debts and payments. And I won't forget everything you've done for me and my family."

"Go on. You're going to make me cry again, and I had enough of that from Charles."

Chapter 28
Drama Queen

I got home that evening, after dropping Ray off, to find Dakota's car in our driveway and the young man himself in the back yard playing fetch with Roby. The traitorous canine was more interested in the sticks Dakota was throwing than in welcoming me home.

Even Dakota wasn't that happy to see me. When he stopped playing with Roby he collapsed into a plastic lawn chair and stared morosely at the house. Evening was falling, and a skein of birds crossed the sky.

In the shadows I got a good look at Dakota. I'm not a detective for nothing. "You spoke to your mother again?"

He nodded. "I went to Wahiawa to see her this afternoon."

"How's she doing?"

"She looks good. They have a prison garden now, growing food that they serve in the kitchens, and she's been working out there. She looks like she did after we spent a week at the Jersey shore, tanned and happy."

"Good for her."

"But how long will it last?" A gust of wind swept through, tossing some dead leaves that had gathered at the base of trees. There was deep emotion in his voice, and I didn't know how to respond. I'd had a pretty emotional day myself.

Roby sat up by Dakota's side, and when there was no stick forthcoming, he rested his head on Dakota's knee and Dakota stroked the soft fur at the top of his golden head.

"I don't know what to say," I finally admitted. "She's a human being, and she deserves the chance to be happy."

"Even after she ruined my life?"

"Excuse me, drama queen," I said. "She knocked a big hole in your life by abandoning you. You had a bad couple of years there. But I'd say you've done a fine job of repairing that hole, finishing high school and college, getting a job. You're never going to be able to forget those bad times, but you've moved on."

The last rays of the dying sun cast a long shard of light across the lawn. "She wasn't exactly mother of year even before she went to prison."

"I know, Dakota. And I know how hard it was for you to trust me and Mike, and to pull yourself up and apply yourself to school when you'd missed so much. But that shows how strong you are. Maybe you can afford to share a bit of that strength with your mother."

"You don't even like her."

I shivered as another cool breeze swept through. "This is not about her and me. There was a time when I wanted her to suffer life in prison because of what she did to you. But that was a long while ago, and she's served her time. She deserves a chance—but she has to do this next part on her own. She's not entitled to drag you down if she falls."

"I told her that today. She cried, Kimo. She said all she wanted in this life was to make it up to me for the time she wasn't there. And I had to nod along and say she was welcome to do that, but I had to see some proof she could stay off drugs before I would let her back in."

"Good for you." I rubbed my upper arms. The conversation was important and I didn't want to disrupt it, but I was getting cold.

"It's all thanks to you and Mike. If you guys hadn't taken me in, I would have ended up no better than her."

"I doubt that." I stood up. "You want a pizza for dinner? I can make a call."

"Can I get anchovies?"

Dakota was the only person I knew who liked anchovies on his pizza. Mike and I both believed that they stunk up the pizza, even if they were only on his part.

"You can have your very own. And take home any leftover slices."

I called Mike. He was on his way home, and he said that if I ordered the pizzas, he'd pick them up. I made the appropriate calls and then went back outside to Dakota, grabbing a lightweight sweater as I went.

"How do you like working at the Albergo?" I asked. "Is the one in Ko Olina as fancy as the one in Kahala?"

"Absolutely. I've been over there a couple of times for training. Everything at that hotel is computerized. The maids have a special code for the doors that registers who went in when and how long they were inside. Management looks at those reports every week. Even the pool boys have to register how many towels come in and out electronically."

I had an idea. "How about the parking lot? Do they register who comes and goes?"

He nodded. "Three separate systems. One for the front entrance and a couple of spots for people who are checking in. Another one for the guest parking lot, and a third for the employee lot. They photograph every license plate and they can track what time I pull into the lot, and then how long it takes me to swipe my access card at the back entrance. Then how long before I get to my position and log in there."

"Go back for a second. They photograph license plates for the guest parking lot? Ins and outs?"

He nodded.

"Jesus, why didn't someone tell us this when we were first looking for Karen Fontenot's car? We could have known right away which one of the two rentals she took."

An automatic light in our neighbor's yard clicked on, casting more shadows on the area around us. I had to catch him up to how initially the family had told us the wrong plate number and we'd wasted a day searching for her.

Then I realized that the day they reported her missing, Leo knew which car would be found at the park. The one in his brother's name, because he had been driving the one in Karen's name.

He had deliberately misled us. "How long do you keep those records?" I asked.

He shrugged. "Don't know. My rotation in IT doesn't start until next month."

While Dakota started playing with Roby again, I went inside and added a couple of notes to my file. First thing Wednesday morning, Ray and I were going out to Kahala to look at those records. The clock was ticking; we had to get this case resolved before Friday, when Doc would issue his death certificate. The Fontenots would be free to take Karen's body back to New Orleans and we'd lose any chance of speaking with the family face to face.

Chapter 29
Surfer

Mike showed up with the pizzas, and we had a nice evening together, which reminded me of when Dakota lived with us, only neither of us had to tell him to do his homework.

Wednesday morning, I picked up Ray and I called the manager of the Albergo in Kahala. They did indeed have computerized records of every car that entered or left the guest parking lot. He was apologetic, but it was company policy to require a warrant to get any of that information. I'd heard that unofficially from Ori, the tennis pro, so I didn't argue.

We drove downtown and parked at headquarters. While Ray caught up with some human resources videos he needed to watch, I prepared the information necessary for a warrant, and then went to Judge Forest's chambers to get him to sign it. We couldn't leave for Kahala until after noon, so we stopped at a Zippy's for lunch.

"I blame your mother-in-law," Ray said as we walked in. "Her Korean fried chicken is one of my very favorite foods."

Ray and Julie had their own relationship with Mike's parents. Dominic and Soon-O attended St. Filomena's Catholic church because they offered Mass in Korean – the same church that Ray and

Julie attended. When Vinnie was born, they had asked Mike to be one of his godfathers.

Since then, Ray had eaten a lot of Soon-O's cooking, though he admitted that Zippy's version of Korean fried chicken couldn't touch Soon-O's. "We'll have to get her to cook some up soon," I said.

We talked as we ate, though until we could verify that someone had taken the second rental car out the morning Karen was killed, it was hard to make a plan for the rest of the day.

Hawai'i is one of nineteen states that require both front and back license plates. So as each car waited for the gate arm to rise, a digital camera snapped a photo of the front plate. Then an OCR program read the plate number and saved the image in a file with the number and the date and time stamp.

It was almost too easy to have one of the guys in the security office pull up the record for both rental cars that Monday morning. Karen's car pulled out of the lot at 7:54 AM. A few cars behind her was the car registered in Jules's name.

The camera was positioned to only photograph the plate, not the driver. But at last we had proof that someone in the family was lying to us.

The guy printed the two photos for us, and we went out to the coffee shop overlooking the pool to think about a plan. Who were we going to approach first?

We bought a couple of over-priced coffees and staked out a terrazzo-topped table in the shade of a pair of arching palm trees. The sun was bright, shimmering off the incoming surf in glittery waves.

"My money is on Leo," I said. "I don't want to start with Belle, because I doubt she was driving, and because she'll protect her sons."

"Not Jules either, because he's an attorney, and he'll throw all kinds of legal problems in front of us," Ray said.

I sipped my coffee. Big Mo's was better, and neither of them were going to replace the Kope Bean in my book. "The kids were buying dope, so barring further information I think that knocks them out."

"And Emeline doesn't strike me as the action type. I'm not even sure that she knows the depth of the family's financial problems."

"Which leaves us with Leo," I said.

Ray picked up his coffee. "How do we isolate him from his family?"

I sat back and looked out at the pool and beach area. There were a number of fine-looking young men out there, mostly pool boys and towel guys. They all wore lightweight white shirts and tropical pattern board shorts.

Most of the male guests were out of shape. They were heavier than they should be, often wearing bathing suits too skimpy for their physiques. A few were even cadaverously old, with stooped shoulders and bony ribs.

Every so often, though, there was a handsome gent who made the vista worthwhile. Straight ahead of me was a fit, tanned guy in his thirties, holding up a six-foot surfboard in a move that was meant to look casual but to me showed he didn't know how to use that board at all.

I eyed his muscular legs, his flat stomach, and his mane of dark hair. If I was ten years younger and single I'd be all over him.

Then he turned to face us, and I realized it was Leo Fontenot, and my initial reaction was yuck.

"I think Leo's solved that problem for us," I said to Ray, and pointed him out. "Shall we go have our chat?"

We got up, still carrying our coffee cups, and walked in his direction. Something in his personal radar caused him to turn and see us, and his mouth dropped open a bit.

Then he took off for the water, carrying the surfboard.

I had to take back what I thought earlier. He ran with the board under his arm with ease. When he reached the water he tossed it into the waves and then jumped on and started paddling furiously.

"You want to go after him?" Ray asked.

"Where's he going to go? The deal about surfing is that you paddle out, and then the waves bring you right back."

"He's not going straight out, though, is he?"

I watched as Leo paddled. No, he wasn't heading straight out to sea; instead he had taken a left turn and was going toward China Walls, an exposed reef break where Koko Head curved out to form a protected bay.

"He's trying to get a wave that will bring him in too far down the shore for us to catch him," I said. "Smart move, but dumb, too."

"Why dumb?" Ray asked, as we moved farther down the sandy beach, keeping an eye on him.

"This time of year, the surf at China Walls is too short to get a good wave. He could end up floundering out there, too far to get brought in. And there are rip currents, too."

I pulled out my phone and called the Ocean Safety division. I gave them Leo's position and the danger he was in, and then my badge number and told them he was wanted in a homicide investigation.

The dispatcher promised to get a boat out to his location ASAP. By then, Leo was almost too far out to see clearly, though I could make out the hunched shape of his body between waves.

"You really are a dumb ass, Leo," I said.

As we watched, he tried to stand up a couple of times but he couldn't keep his balance. The third time he went off the board entirely and we lost sight of him.

"Come on, Leo, get back on the board."

In the distance I heard the roar of an outboard engine, and the Ocean Safety boat came into view. "Can you see Leo?" I asked Ray.

"Just the board, once in a while. You?"

"Same. There are rip currents out there. He could get caught in one and swept past Koko Head."

We saw Ocean Safety approach the area where we'd last seen Leo's board, and they cut their engines. A guy stood on the prow with binoculars scanning the area as another one grappled the board onto the boat.

"We cannot go back to Belle Fontenot and tell her another one of her children is missing,' I said. "I refuse to do that. Come on, Leo."

The guy on the prow seemed to have spotted someone or something, because he waved to the helmsman and they moved a bit farther inshore. The spotter kept peering into his glasses, waving the boat forward.

Then they were all moving quickly. One guy jumped into the ocean and another leaned over the side of the boat. It was hard to see clearly from so far away, but it looked like they were lifting someone on board.

I called Ocean Rescue again, identified myself and asked for the dispatcher. "The boat that just picked up a surfer," I said. "Where are they taking him? I need to talk to him."

"Hold for a moment."

When the hold music came on, I nearly snorted with laughter, as the Beach Boys invited me to go surfing because everybody was learning how. "At least someone in this office has a sense of humor."

"Where is their base?" Ray asked.

"They've got an office at Hanauma Bay. That's probably where they'll take him."

As the boat revved its engines and started back out to sea, Ray and I turned to walk back to where I'd parked. "Detective?" the voice on the phone asked.

"Yes, sir?"

"The victim is being taken to Hanauma Bay."

"Victim?"

"I'm afraid you won't be able to question him. The EMT on the boat pronounced him dead."

I thanked the dispatcher and turned to Ray. "Change of plans. We need to speak to Belle."

Chapter 30
What Remains

We trudged back up the sand to the pool area, to the tune of a light reggae beat coming from loudspeakers. David and Jessica Fontenot were lounging in the spa pool with fruity drinks. "You're going to want come upstairs with us," I said.

"Why? What's up? Why did Uncle Leo take off down the beach?"

"Your uncle didn't make it back. We need to go up and let your family know."

Jessica started to cry. "This is the worst vacation ever! First Aunt Karen and now Uncle Leo. I want to go home!"

Her brother put a dripping arm around her shoulder and encouraged her to stand up. Gently he wrapped her in a towel. Then he downed the rest of his drink and rubbed his shoulders dry. He picked up his shirt and his sister's beach wrap and got her to step into her rubber sandals.

The wind picked up, shaking the palm trees in an agitated hula, and the lifeguards began motioning people in from the water. If we'd arrived a few minutes later, or managed to keep Leo from hitting the waves, he'd still be alive.

David spoke quietly to his sister, trying to calm her down, but she kept sobbing. Eventually she was quiet enough that the two of them could follow Ray and me to the elevator.

"What happened?" David asked as we waited. "He was a pretty good surfer. He spent a lot of time in Mexico. He even surfed Puerto Escondido, which has monster waves."

"According to him," Jessica sniffled. "He probably sat on the beach and got high."

"I can't say for certain, but it looked like he went too far out, maybe got caught by a rip current."

"Where is he?" Jessica asked.

"The Ocean Safety patrol will take him to their outpost at Hanauma Bay. From there he'll be transported to the medical examiner's office."

"Not the same people who have Aunt Karen?" David demanded.

"The same. But I think your aunt will be released shortly."

We rode the elevator up in silence, and then Ray and I followed David and Jessica to Belle's suite. We knocked and no one answered.

"Maybe she's in ours," David said. We went a few steps down the hall and he used his key card to open the door to the suite he and his sister shared with their parents.

Jules and Belle sat at a table by the window, deep in conversation. When they looked up and saw us, Jules said, "Not now. We're busy."

Ray stepped up. "I'm sorry, but we have bad news. Leo Fontenot took a surfboard out into the ocean a short while ago and paddled too far out for safety. Ocean Safety was called, and they picked him up." He hesitated for a moment. "He didn't survive."

"Didn't survive?" Jules demanded. "What does that mean?"

"It means he's dead," Belle said sharply. "Didn't your expensive education teach you that much?"

Jessica started to cry again, and her brother bundled her off to what I assumed was the bedroom they shared.

"The waves are tricky this time of year," I said. "The farther out you go, the harder it is to pick up a big wave that will bring you back to shore. We saw him floundering, falling off his board."

"What were you doing watching him?" Jules demanded.

"You might not know, but there's a camera system at the gate to the guest parking lot that takes photos of license plates as cars go in and out."

"What does that have to do with my question?"

I stayed calm. There was no use getting agitated with Jules Fontenot. "We had a judge issue a warrant this morning so we could review the license plates of the cars that left the hotel at the time your sister did."

"We've already been through this. She took the wrong car."

"Yes. But someone else left in the other car four minutes after she did."

"Who? Who else would have taken that car?

"Leo," Belle said resignedly. "I knew he did it, I just couldn't believe it."

Jules looked at his mother, clearly not understanding her.

"It's the damn money," Belle said. "Which you and your brother have been harassing me about."

She looked up at us. "This vacation was going to be my last hurrah, my last big expense. I was using a debit card against my investment account, and the money ran out more quickly than I expected."

She frowned. "Unfortunately the Fontenot family has a long history of spending more than they earned, and it's finally caught up with us." Her shoulders drooped. "When we get back to New Orleans I'll be living on my husband's social security payment."

"But surely Terre Riche is worth money," I said.

"Which is why my sons want to sell it. They promised me a unit in the new condos they want to build. One for Karen and Charles, too, but she refused. She didn't want to take Charles away from Terre Riche. She thought that would be too difficult for him."

"Don't say anything more, mother."

"I'll say what I please." She stamped her cane on the carpet, which didn't have quite the effect I thought she wanted. "I was stuck, detective. I knew that we couldn't go on as we have been, but I raised three very stubborn children. Jules and Leo needed Karen's signature as well as my own to sell Terre Riche. The boys hoped that they could convince her during this trip."

Jules put his head in his hands. "I never dreamed he would go so far."

Belle looked at us. "What happened?"

Ray and I were still standing by the door, and it didn't look like we were going to be invited to sit. "Charles told us that he saw his mother and Leo arguing on the mountain path before he wandered off to look for leaves."

"I'd tear him apart if he went on the witness stand," Jules snarled.

"Which is why we knew we needed more evidence," Ray said.

"My foster son works at another location of the Albergo and he told me about the license plate photos. We were planning to speak with all of you today to find out who took the car out when Leo ran."

"Your medical examiner won't take another week to release Leo's body, will he?" Belle asked.

"No, ma'am. We can get the autopsy expedited."

"Good. I want to leave here on Friday with what remains of my family."

Chapter 31
Grounded

While I drove us back to headquarters, Ray verified that Ocean Safety had transferred Leo Fontenot to the ME's office. He called there and had a happy reunion with Alice Kanamura and then Doc himself. Doc promised that he would expedite the autopsy because he wanted both the Fontenots out of his facility quickly.

When we met with Sampson, it felt like a letdown. We'd solved the case, but at a terrible cost, and we didn't even have an admission of guilt, just a fool who fled on a surfboard into waves he couldn't handle.

"How do you know for certain that the older brother didn't do it?" Sampson asked.

"Charles identified Leo as arguing with his mother on the mountain. The only thing we don't know, and we'll never know, is if he pushed her, or she fell on her own."

Sampson steepled his fingers. "I can't tell Doc Takayama what to put on the death certificate, and neither can you. But death by misadventure would be better for the department and the family."

"In both cases," I said, and Ray nodded. "We'll talk to Doc once he finishes the autopsy on Leo."

"There's still a lot of paperwork to fill out. Go to it."

As we walked back to our desks, I said, "Go you. Less than a week back on the force and already solved a big crime."

"Teamwork, brah," he said, and he held out his fingers in a shaka.

That night over dinner I told Mike what had happened. "I feel terrible for Belle," I said. "To have lost her daughter, and then her son."

"You were surprised that I wanted to join QOLE," he said. "Starting when the twins were born, I realized that it's more important to be honest and open with people. Watching you, listening to the questions the kids have. My parents always taught me to be honest, and I guess I still want their approval. I want to be a good son."

"The way that Dakota wants to be to Angelina."

"Yeah, that's something we're going to have to accept. Angelina Gianelli becoming part of our ohana, coming to family luaus."

"Hey, let's not get ahead of ourselves. She still has to prove herself to Dakota."

The next afternoon, Doc's office notified us that he was releasing both Leo's and Karen's bodies to the family, which had asked that they be cremated. The verdict in both cases was death by misadventure.

I sat back in my chair and looked at Ray. "I should be glad to close two cases, but I still have mixed feelings," I said. "Do you think it's beyond our jurisdiction to call the family and ask what's going to happen to Charles now?"

"Maybe ours, but not Jimmy's," Ray said. "Why don't you call him?"

I did.

"Charles Fontenot's grandmother showed up at the hospital this morning with her daughter-in-law," Jimmy said. "The hospital notified me and I spoke with Mrs. Belle Fontenot."

"What are they going to do with Charles?"

"Technically, his legal guardian should be his father, but Omari

Fontenot has agreed to let Charles's grandmother take the lead in Charles's care, as long as he retains visiting rights. Charles will be going home with them to New Orleans. The family is putting their property up for sale, and the way the deed is structured, part of the proceeds of any sale will go into a trust fund for Charles. His grandmother wants to follow his mother's wishes and send him to a residential treatment center in Chicago."

I thanked Jimmy, told him to take care, and hung up. "Well, that's him sorted," I said. "I hope they get the money together so he's there whenever the winter term starts in January."

"About schools," Ray said, twirling a pencil between his fingers. "Last night we got a call from your friend Terri Hirsch. Seems she sits on the scholarship committee for Punahou."

"I'm not surprised. She engineered a scholarship for Dakota to go there, and picked up whatever Mike and I couldn't afford."

"She says there's a fund for the children of law enforcement personnel that Vinnie could apply for. You ever heard of that?"

I shook my head. "But Dakota's been out of there for five years now."

"You think she's doing this just for us?"

"Her first husband Eric was a cop. So she's always been concerned about cops and their families. But if she's doing it just for Vinnie, what does it matter? She's part of our ohana, just like you and Julie. We look out for each other."

"I don't want him to grow up spoiled and entitled."

I looked at him. "You mean like me? My brothers? My kids?"

"No, I didn't mean that. It's just, you see how hard it is for kids these days. So many more of them have behavioral problems, like Charles. Or they get accustomed to privilege, like David and Jessica Fontenot. How do I make sure Vinnie grows up properly?"

"You do everything you can for him, and hope for the best. You give him a good education, for one thing. I'm not saying he won't learn in the public schools. Mike graduated from Farrington and he's done fine for himself. But Vinnie and Addie and Owen are friends, and if they go to different schools they'll be separated." I smiled. "And I want Vinnie around to keep my kids grounded, like you do for me."

Then we heard Sampson's voice booming. "Donne, Kanapa'aka, new homicide. You're up."

And we were.

Acknowledgments

The usual suspects get their thanks here. Randall Klein has become my editor of choice, working on all kinds of books for me, and always doing a terrific job to help me tell better stories. Kelly Nichols once again has come through with a terrific cover, no matter how much I delay and badger her and ask for changes. Stacey Ducker is keeping me on track as my very able assistant.

Thanks to Pam Reinhardt for New Orleans advice. Any mistakes I have made are my own, for the sake of the story. My Hawaiian ohana is always there to ask questions—Cindy Chow and Annette Mahon, for starters. The amazing author James O. Born took time out from his busy schedule to answer some questions about the Miranda warning. Thank you to child psychologist Eileen Matluck for help with Charles's behavior; she appears here in two guises, under her own name and as Dr. Leenie.

Interested in the details of Kimo's life in Hawai'i? Check out Amanda Cooks and Styles for a recipe for the grilled beef skewers he makes. Remember to allow time for marinating! https://amandacooksandstyles.com/hawaiian-beef-skewers/

Readers I meet are often surprised that there is a real subgenre for Hawaiian music. I encourage you to check out some of Kimo's and my favorites: Keola Beamer, Paula Fuga, Hapa, and Kalani Pe'a.

I appreciate the help of my beta readers: Tim Brehme, Sally Huxley, Nancy Ann Gazo, and Andy Jackson. Any remaining errors are my responsibility alone!

A special thank you to Broward College, which has provided me with four sabbatical terms over the course of twenty years, during which time I have been able to read, write, research and travel. None of this would be possible without the support of my loving husband Marc and our two furry children, Brody and Griffin, and all the readers who have written or spoken to me about what Kimo means to them.

Thanks for reading! I'd love to stay in touch with you. Subscribe to one or more of my newsletters: Gay Mystery and Romance or Golden Retriever Mysteries and I promise I won't spam you!

Follow me at Goodreads to see what I'm reading, and my author page at Facebook where I post news and giveaways.

Learn more about Mahu Investigations Series:

You'll fall instantly in love with Kimo, from his scrupulous approach to his job to his easy way with his nieces, nephews, brothers, and friends, even when some turn against him on his new path. What's happening to him is the late-breaking realization that he's gay. If he's going to accept that and live as he's meant to, he has to upend everything and learn a whole new culture. It's a rocky path, and that's what makes a good story. Author Plakcy, creator of The Golden Retriever Mysteries, weaves a very different kind of tale here —realistic and hard-boiled, yet also empathetic and warm. **MAHU is a taut, ingenious, many-threaded mystery, each unexpected plot twist leading believably to the next, yet nothing telegraphed—in other words, an extremely satisfying read.**

The entire series is here: https://amzn.to/3Gokhsa

Looking for something new to read? Neil has a series just for you!

The Golden Retriever Mysteries? You'll find the entire series here: https://amzn.to/3Kki7w6

Author of over 50 romance and mystery novels and short story collections. **Neil's entire catalog of books are here:** https://amzn.to/3I7qOIf

About the Author

NEIL S. PLAKCY is the author of over fifty mystery and romance novels, including the best-selling golden retriever mysteries and the highly acclaimed *Mahu* series, a three-time finalist for the Lambda Literary Awards. His stories have been featured in numerous venues, including the Bouchercon anthology Florida Happens and Malice Domestic's Murder Most Conventional and several Happy Homicides collections.

He is a professor of English at Broward College in South Florida, where he lives with his husband and their rambunctious golden retrievers.

His website is www.mahubooks.com.

www.ingramcontent.com/pod-product-compliance
Lightning Source LLC
LaVergne TN
LVHW012017060526
838201LV00061B/4342